A Place to Return

Tales of Love

I0452190

Henry Greenfield

Also by Henry Greenfield
Available through First Champvert Press
9016 SW 215 Terrace
Cutler Bay, Florida 33189
greenfie@hotmail.com for autographed orders

Second Time Around
The Rabbi's Girl
Desperate Conspiracy
Echoes from The Friendship Club

First Champvert Press Edition, 2013

This is a work of fiction. Some characters have traits of people the author knows. The narrative is not intended to portray real events. The novel is not intended to be autobiographical, nor should it be taken as such.

ISBN-13: 978-0615918150 (First Champvert Press)
ISBN-10: 0615918158

This book is dedicated to Miami Jackson's English
Department and the students who walk
the pages of memory

Chapter One

As she read the personal data, the Vice President twisted a red pen through her fingers like a schoolmarm readying for mistakes. Herb Rizer watched her circle his date of birth and the blank space for religious preference. She must have overlooked his rapid rise to supervisor at Hunter College. "Holy heavens of God," the interviewer said, "your commending dean surely knows one must pay his dues." Youth and faith affected job performance in Lola May Ferringer's view, Herb thought, and pictured her in a pantsuit instead of a billowy dress with garish red hibiscus on a lavender background and a red kerchief around her neck to hide her jowls. She stared at his application as if the problem which took up chair-space in front of her would leave of its own volition.

Her office had no degrees hung anywhere. An autographed portrait of Boman F. Ashe, University of Miami's founder, was a grainy blowup poorly colorized and lost on otherwise bare walls. What was the delay? Shit, an associate registrar at Hunter College inside of a year, Herb had come home to an ailing dad. Were his skills at registration, scheduling, recording, posting, reporting, billing, and such too implausible for one so young? Had his undergraduate degree from the University of Miami denigrated his standing in the world of academia? Were University of Miami's baccalaureates so plebeian that his alma mater looked askance at hiring one? What about his masters degree, magna cum laude, from Columbia? Didn't that best a third-rate Bachelor of Arts?

Lola Mae's forearms triangulated above his accolades, a double chin rested atop clasped hands, and breasts pressed a laminated blond desk with a plastic nameplate, Miss Lola May Ferringer, Vice President. She stared at some point in the ceiling that made Herb want to look and doodled on his paperwork. Was he to change his Aquarian birth date? "My," she began, "twenty-four is quite, how shall I say, impressive for this list of achievements."

"Did you receive Dr. Newman's recommendation?" he asked.

Miss Ferringer flipped through the file but removed nothing. "I paid my dues at the county board of education before working here as an aide to Dr. Ashe," she said to the ceiling.

Herb winced at the *good old boys club* reference that friends said was on the wane in South Florida. Both U of M deans, Alvarez and Bitter, assured him that with outstanding achievements, he was a natural for the registrar opening. Surely Ferringer overcame that old boy's club exclusivity prerequisite for her job as VP. He wondered if her rise had been through coaching which, with few exceptions, was a usual track to administration. Many executives had degrees in physical education and/or had coached major sports including the U of M's current president, Dr. Beaumont. Nonetheless, he believed that liberal arts degrees were more than paper and so went headlong into his background, "The school of music, my first major, under Dr. Beaumont and Chancellor Gray ranks among the best in the South. Dean Bitter as well as Dean Alvarez know my work—we coordinated programs between Columbia and this fine institution. The deans recommended that I toss my hat in for registrar. "

"Both of them highly recommended you." She slid the material aside and looked for a while at the wall photo of Dr. Ashe. "He was a fine gentleman, God rest his soul, a true Southerner. What is your nationality?" the VP asked. Her wandering stare now fixed on him.

He wanted to answer Lithuanian because Dean Alvarez's secretary said he looked like the actor Lawrence Harvey, but answered, "American."

Ferringer looked away as if she hadn't any patience for tricky answers. "No," she said, "I mean your ancestral nationality?"

"I was born and raised in Miami."

"Rizer is a somewhat familiar name."

"My parents are not unknown."

She stood, back to him, and peered out at the campus commons. "Oh, yes—"

"My dad sponsored war refugees."

"—gambling and nightclubs on Miami Beach."

"He built and ran hotels. The Roney, Beau Rivage, Eden Roc. His Five O'clock Club brought in celebrity entertainers in the twenties."

"—and I recall a trial for murder—Meyer Lansky, the mob, and all that unpleasant history."

"Before I was born."

Ferringer turned, knuckles now pressed on her desk, and leaned toward him like a prosecuting attorney. "Isn't Rizer a Jewish name?"

"We're members of Temple Emanu-El."

"Isn't that a Jewish Church?" She eased back into her chair.

The testimony from the witness stand remained restrained. "A synagogue."

Ferringer slowly slipped Herb's file toward the trash beside her chair. "You all certainly built an extravagant church for yourselves."

"Are religious affiliation and age the only slants on your decision making?"

"Sakes alive, I think this interview has concluded. We haven't any position here befitting you. Thank you for coming."

Did Lola May Ferringer offer her hand? You bet not. When Herb rose, he reached across to her as she sat erect, slid back, and emphasized, "That will be all, Mr. Rizer."

Clasping his hands together in an ironic gesture, Herb smiled broadly, shrugged, and walked out into a terrazzo and glass lobby where staff registrars and bursars, aids, and scholarship personnel harried students about records, grades, fees, course offerings, financial aid, housing, credit hours, and schedule conflicts. Herb heard the vice president call,

"Close the door, young man," as he headed for the stairs and the dean's office. Three at a time, he bounded up the steps and at the third-floor landing, took off his suede blazer, loosened his silk tie, and rolled up his sleeves. Seeing his reflection in glass, he fixed the part in his brown hair.

The secretary who kidded Herb about being a Lawrence Harvey look alike loved *The Manchurian Candidate*. Herb reminded her that the actor did not have blue eyes and unlike his own pockmarked cheeks, Harvey's complexion was silver-screen smooth. She countered with the Rizers surely were Lithuanian and distantly related to Lawrence Harvey. "Check your family tree," she advised. Her vision was myopic in Herb's estimation. For her last birthday, though, he had rented the *Manchurian Candidate* and a sixteen millimeter projector for her private showing. Greeting aside, she let the dean know that Lawrence Harvey was in the outer office. Abraham Alvarez welcomed Herb.

"Hired?" he asked as Herb sat in front of another laminated blond desk, this one with a carved wood nameplate, Maximilian Alvarez, Dean of Arts and Sciences.

"Would Governor Faubus hire William Shatner?"

"She's an old maid with Southern hangups. Show her your ham hocks and chick peas. I will speak with her."

"I'm afraid, Max, that the university's Eustis harpy believes Jews have horns."

The dean, graying at the temples decked by his horn-rimmed glasses, leaned back with his hairy fingers clasped behind his head. "You are too sensitive, Herb, my young friend."

"I went to New York because this town less than a generation ago posted its biases, 'No dogs, no Jews, no Niggers.'"

"Your father's contemporaries bought out the Kennelworth Hotel and the anti-Semites."

"Yeah, ownership changed but not hearts and minds."

Max Alvarez flashed a gold Star of David from beneath the knot in his blue and red striped tie. He seemed to enjoy flashing the graying hair on his chest. "She'd have subjected me to her dislike then."

The emblem of Judaism reminded Herb of a joke. "Did I tell you about Dracula hunched over a beautiful sleeping virgin?"

"Not another one."

"She's startled awake and grabbed for a cross around her neck."

"This better not be an ethnic one, Herb."

"Dracula says to her as his Mogen David Star falls out, 'Dat don't make no difference to me.'"

Alvarez smiled then said, "I do not get it."

"Jeez, Max. I thought the Jewish accent was convincing."

"It sounded Lithuanian." Herb laughed. Alvarez continued, "Listen, my friend. You're the right guy for that registrar's job, but it's not my decision. The adjunct position in English is still open, if you wish."

"That's why I'm here."

"The first full time teaching job to open is yours, you know."

"Thanks, Max."

"Your dad came through for me. It is my turn. The secretary will process your paperwork."

"What if the department head isn't okay with this?"

"I'll send him off to Castro. Join me for a drink at Compadres and we'll have dinner afterward."

"What time?"

"Sixish. Wear tight pants."

"How about my treat at Friar Tuck's. Ira Sullivan plays Friday nights and the bar draws girls for free drinks on week nights."

"Compadres has a Judy Garland impersonator and fabulous male strippers."

"Do I still get the adjunct job if I say, *no thanks*?"

"Better you not offend an academic dean and your boss."

"Six then with tight pants."

With a temporary faculty identification in hand, Herb visited the English Department and introduced himself to the secretary. The department head wasn't available, but a wispy blond who taught American Lit volunteered to show him around. She acted reticent except to point out a conference room, faculty offices, men and ladies rooms, copy center, computer room, professional library, kitchen replete with fridge, microwave, and vending machines. Damn if her hair, which swayed across her back, wasn't a natural without dark, telltale roots. She seemed almost as tall as Herb which put her close to six feet in stiletto heels. Her diaphanous print shuffled around undergarments like a stepsister awaiting a godmother to transform her best clothes into a formal gown and glass slippers. As far as glamorous, Beth Shockett wore no makeup and didn't need any. He asked if she liked jazz and just as coincidence comes ashore like waves, Ira Sullivan turned out to be a favorite. The invite to Friar Tuck's got a "love to," once she gave him an eye to eye exam and a quick perusal of the potentially buff package under sporty clothes. She appeared early thirties, he guessed, and wondered who in the department overlooked this grad school chick who likely paid her tuition by dancing at the Pussycat Theater. Jeez, was it that he'd reread *Streetcar* and Blanche Dubois fixed in mind that caused him to believe this fair blond, coincidently, didn't mind age differences? Beth Shockett, an older woman and a recent divorcee, seemed to like him, and Herb Rizer, undoubtedly, liked her. She appeared attracted to Lawrence Harvey. So what if he'd been wrong about the fair hiring practices for the registrar job and felt too keenly about connecting romantically. He hadn't dated since the Bergdorf Goodman model fiasco and hadn't any barometer for foul weather with Beth.

Chapter Two

After Pompano almondine with the dean at Chart House and a quick and uncomfortable cocktail at Compadres, Herb picked up Beth Shockett. She lived near Friar Tucks, and he asked if she might walk with him through the Grove to the bar, but she begged off because, being early evening, there was a possibility people who were unaware of her recent divorce might be out and about. Well, her honesty certainly cleared up the being overlooked in school supposition. Within minutes, they were luckily in a hard-to-come-by parking space on Main Street across from the night spot and inside before their chit-chat moved beyond generality. He'd learned she dabbled with oils, liked the artist Egon Schiele and expressionists, and thought J.D. Salinger was the voice of her generation. The crowded bar had a beery odor which the circular cooling vents on the galvanized tile ceiling forced out through the front entrance. Walking into that scent was the only thing Herb didn't like about the place. With Beth, he passed a mini-skirted chick at the bar poking the guy next to her in the ribs, and he, turning away, fisted peanuts and began feeding them to a flaming redhead beside him. At ease with his arm around Beth's waist, he led her around the dancers on the floor. She placed her arm around him. The ruckus of post happy-hour jabbering, clanking of glasses, canned music, scraping of chairs, laughter, high-spirited singing negated conversation. They passed a chalkboard above the bar on which someone, probably the manager, had scrawled in fuchsia script, "No Ira Sullivan tonight."

Perhaps if Ira Sullivan's non appearance had been on the billboard outside, Beth would have cancelled as well. Disappointment cooled her glow in the muted light of a redwood stained, pine-planked floor across which her stiletto heels clacked in time with the canned clarinet solo, likely Pete Fountain's improvisation of "Moon Glow." Anticipating a suggestion to go, Herb led her to a booth that surrounded them with maroon padding and diagonal redwood veneer planks. Herb felt guilty of a date on false pretenses—no Ira Sullivan.

Beth fingered initials that were carved into the cedar, *B.S.*, and he wondered if, in fact, she'd been at this very table previously. Is this where her husband proposed? Where he dumped her? The audience applauded a pianist ascending the stage. It was a musician-friend who agreed to fill in for Sullivan. Neither Herb nor Beth believed they listened to George Shearing at less than twenty paces. "Days of Wine and Roses," started the evening off as well as the delivery of two Southern Comfort Manhattans which went down easily. She applauded Shearing and started a standing ovation at the end of his set.

"My *ex* hated bar scenes," she offered after the glow returned.

"Hope that isn't a *ditto* for you," he said wondering about his thing for mystical blonds, women on the rebound, and women getting dumped by a spouse. How recently he'd been dumped came back despite attempts to forget Mary. Ah, yes, dumped by Mary. Traveling to Minnesota to marry his New York flame, Herb met her natural-blond parents who had proven to be a nightmare. His marriage proposal had been set aside with their Christian insistence on a compatible husband for their Lutheran daughter. Mary's parents had circled the religious preference space on Herb's application. Evidently Minnesota and Ferringer weren't open to his Judaism. How naive not to see an unraveling of Herb's and Mary's emotional knot. Had Beth's *ex* unraveled their knot as callously at this very table?

"Let's dance," she said. He liked her straightforwardness. Without an answer, she took his hand and drew close to him in the magic of a slow encounter on a not quite empty dance floor. Dionne Warwick sang "Love Power." Beth felt soft and willing. The Manhattan relaxed him for the enticing moves. She glided as though she'd choreographed his fox trot. Herb used a hip to hip side-step in his dance that came naturally to Beth as she back-stepped

8

and dipped, twirled and came back better than Minnesota Mary with whom he'd practiced endlessly for such smoothness. Long hair brushed his hand, and she moved her warm cheek against his. Some people seem challenged by a first dance, but Herb and Beth came to an easiness as naturally as moonlight over Miami. She pressed to him as if they were alone. Did she hear his crying heart? Sense the tingling wherever her palms lighted? Feel the sweetness of his arousal? Was the gentle sway and her cheek, soft against his, drawing him from past fear to present trust? From disenchantment to anticipation? Did a rub of bodies, parts soft and tamable, others tense and drawn, still others hungry and alluring, charm him? If not, why would he remember her easy steps, and a stylistic rendition of "Love Power" well into his life? Why hear the swish of her sexy rayon on his temptable gaberdine during nocturnal fantasies? Why did change come despite coward-like unwillingness? By the time he led her back to another round of Manhattans and a redwood booth, he was no longer the Herb that had walked into Friar Tuck's earlier that evening.

Chapter Three

At a faculty shindig to commemorate the close of a long, hot summer, Beth acted as if she and Herb hadn't dated and declined his offer to dance. She sat at the dean's table teasing a chocolate mousse and looking like a lighthouse beacon on a dark horizon. She'd arrived with some swishy grammarian, a shallow-voiced, tenured prof, who, besides acting aloof, was up for department head while the old standby took a sabbatical. From her date, the More-Important-than-Thou Professor, came no, "Good luck with Freshmen composition," or any acknowledgment that Herb worked in the department. He, unfortunately, sat across from Lola May Ferringer, Vice President of Bigotry, administrative hostess for Dr. Beaumont's *newcomers* table. In her genteel machinations to make everyone feel included, she ignored the sole Jew. Sadly enough if he stared at Beth, the Eustis harpy would be in his direct line of sight, and he'd feel obligated to return her intermittent hate stares.

Dr. Beaumont's speech received warm applause, and each newcomer stood when recognized. Young women seemed taken by wedding-band wearing beaus. Other women were ancient to dead. Herb listened to the piano, bass, and drum trio play fox trots, waltzes, and cha-chas while he wondered how soon, tactfully, to take off. If Max Alvarez hadn't made rounds and introduced him, the welcome dinner would've remained full of strange faces. The dean offered Herb his companion, a mannish girl's physical education instructor, for a dance or two, and so she and Herb shuffled to the tune of "Chapel in the Moonlight," sung by the standard-issue pianist with an operatic baritone voice. Actually, the woman moved as if dancing were outside of her curriculum.

During "Hush, Hush, Sweet Charlotte," the PE gal pulled Lola May Ferringer, likely on her way to the powder room, into a triplet fox trot. When the butch-ess bowed out, the VP seemed mortified to the core. Herb closed the corpulent distance between them. The flabby arms applied a genteel resistance but for the sake of appearance, social grace, and classy breeding, they eventually condescended to the smooth steps of mismatched boy and matron, Jew and Christian, heretic and believer. "My," she began, "you dance quite well, Mr. Rizer."

"My cotillion grooming."

"Lord, I haven't danced since–since, I can not remember when."

"Polished dancers outlast their absence from the floor, dear Miss Ferringer."

"Heavens, do you think this song will go on too very much longer?"

"How unpleasant."

"In my wildest imagination, I saw you go back to Yankee town, not teaching on my campus, not salaried on this turf."

"Life's spiteful."

"Who hired you, if I may ask?"

"Dr. Beaumont."

"I declare. I had no idea you knew him."

"A friend of the family."

"Will you escort me from the floor, please." She indicated a path back to the welcome table.

Herb fox trotted her toward her goal. "Is my job here in jeopardy now?"

In hushed tones, she said as close to his ear as she felt comfortable, "Land of Goshen, unless you give us a reason that you are other than virtuous, honorable, sociable, dedicated, and competent, I would think not." Her face flushed. "I trust you have those virtues."

He nodded.

"The last employee I sent packing, Mr. Rizer, displayed moral impropriety."

"In what way?"

The song ended and people clapped. "I'm sure that is none of your affair, sir."

"Is there a faculty handbook on moral propriety?"

"Step over its fine line, and you'll surely find out."

"Is that a threat, Miss Ferringer?"

"Just fair warning, Mr. Rizer."

He led her back to the welcome table, but as he pulled out a gentlemanly chair, she walked off to wherever had her fancy before the dance. Now free to encounter whomever, he glanced across at Dean Alvarez's table where Beth sat. That coy feline, aware of a favorable glance from Herb, purred for and nuzzled into her escort, a man uneasy around cats and likely used to a pet fish at best. Beth's eyes danced about except at the antsy newcomer looking for an opening to dance her away from the interim department head sucking up to the dean beside him. When she went for a cocktail, Herb went to the bar where he slapped down cash to cover her drink. There was no recognition that he stood there as she sidestepped to the lobby, unabashedly sipped his can-we-talk drink, chatted with a faculty dowager near the exit, and then sauntered out.

Beyond the gabled portico, a sliver of moon lit a long circular drive. A hedge of goldenrod led him to a pathway through the philodendrons and squat pony palms. Why he ducked into the tropical foliage seemed more destiny than reason. From beneath the canopy of a mammoth gumbo limbo, he heard a plaintive sigh and, like one of Odysseus's men, became enchanted. When he neared the bower, a soft hand guided him. Moonlight flecked long, golden hair beneath this canopy of pleasure. Crickets chittered a magic refrain. The balmy air smelled of night blooming jasmine. He sensed dewdrops slipping from the ladened leaves. Beneath his feet, the earth yielded as tenderly as a lover's heart. Was her straightforwardness composing this night's love song? Was the tongue which parted his lips as warm as her heart? Yearning palms journeyed her soft, silk adorned body. Harmonizing with their embrace, a tenor solo from inside, . . . *I've hungered for your kiss, a long, lonely time.* This was a singular moment for him, and he hoped it was for her. He wanted to say *I love you,* but instead hummed along with the melody. *I need your love, God speed your love. . . .* Beth placed a hand over his lips. All she said was, "Meet me at my place in the Grove," and was gone.

While she poured wine in the kitchen, Herb stood in the open doorway to her bedroom. His first view was a half wrinkled spread and one rumpled pillow on a double bed. The unused side had a couple of books and stacked magazines. What disgruntled man had deserted this love nest? No sign of him remained in the hand carved Mayan fertility goddesses around the living room. Two statuesque earth-mothers, stone carved and pregnant, adorned slatted, fruit crates on either side of a plum-cushioned rattan sofa. A ritual mask carved in teak or mahogany hung beside a black vinyl beanbag chair. Stacks of paperbacks: *The Sound and The Fury, The Power and the Glory, All the King's Men, Invisible Man, Exodus, Confessions of Nat Turner, Catcher in the Rye, Five Smooth Stones, Go Tell it on the Mountain,* and others sat on a plank supported by CBS blocks beside the chair. From their condition, they'd obviously been read and reread. Herb flipped through Ellison's *Invisible Man* and checked some of the penciled-in notes–*surreal dream sequence, theft of light–underground symbols*. Infant to post toddler photos of a child splayed artistically on an opposite wall. Either Beth as a child or a younger sister, he speculated. In a dramatic oil which left little white space hanging beside the front door, the girl-child eclipsed an angular woman done in angry stokes of bold cobalt, azure, brown, and crimson. The little girl's complexion seemed fresh while the woman's was ghoulish. The child's eyes afire, she leered at a woman grotesquely twisted away with her eyes cast downward. Herb decided that a psyche prof would fancy a look see. Other paintings, smaller in size, contained nudes, sensual though distorted—violent shapes—all done in an expressionist style with primal colors.
When Beth served him a glass of deep, red wine, it seemed true to a dominant hue in her paintings. The wine's bouquet indulged his senses. She served from a tray with a non-labeled bottle. They swirled and sipped. It had to be a

Bordeaux. The emerald green bottle she set down on a crate beside the beanbag was one he'd painted in a still life, *Wine with Fruit*, now hidden in a closet where no mortal could attest to his lack of talent on canvass. His dabbling in oils created respect for what Beth had accomplished artistically. She set her glass down and drew her legs up like one of her fertility goddesses. He mimicked her furrowed brow.

Some time ago while he'd stood in the bedroom doorway, she had slipped into jeans and a long-sleeved pullover. The deep plum of it matched the cushions on the sofa. When she lifted her hair from the collar, he realized that she wasn't wearing a bra. Her bare feet had purple nail polish, the fair skin of which contrasted with the deep blue denim. He wondered if nude, she'd appear fairer than her ankles. Trying to appear nonchalant, to not stare, to not be rude must have seemed forced for she followed with, "Relax, lover. You're acting as if I'm the first." She raised her top overhead and let it fall onto the floor. Her flaxen hair settled around her shoulders and fell into natural clefts of a Grecian body.

Her matter-of-fact nudity seemed model-like. Finished posing for an artist who wished now to taste reality, he'd set his pallet down beside the completed *Nude with Wine.* Her gentle smile warranted a tribute, homage, affirmation of beauty, but Herb stammered, "God, you're so—you're . . ."

"My ex took himself too seriously." She tossed her straight hair around. Her breasts swayed rhythmically. "Make me laugh." Her blue eyes glistened.

"You say that to all the boys."

She laughed. "Touch me."

He slid onto his knees before a beanbag which contoured her folded legs and lean rump. He wished to bury his face in Galatea, but instead, like a sculptor uncertain of his next cut, he set the pinnacles of his finger on her midriff and then let his palm take in the warmth of her flesh. Herb Rizer at the foot of his fantasies. The moment played in his mind like a vision of beauty wished for but not yet formed. He willed correctness. *Nude with Wine.* His awkwardness

14

drifted away as she followed the lifeline of his palm, moved it to her cheek, then kissed it. Beth Shockett, Professor of American Lit, led him to this creation, and he anticipated an end to his recently muddled engagement.

Their lips met and parted, and they gazed at each other as if he silently honored Aphrodite. He envisioned that which eluded him so many times with Mary and other girls. Beth was the first to speak, "Herb, do you believe minds can superimpose?"

"I never thought about it, but why not?"

She urged his shirt from his waist and unbuttoned it, slid her hands under the shoulders, and let it drop. She placed her palms on his chest. "You're so silky." She slid against him. "Please, please, don't use me," she whispered.

They kissed, easy, pleasing. Her palm brushed his pockmarked cheek, and he turned away. She spread his belt and opened his pants, then guided them to the floor. Her hands explored. He slid her jeans down. A ruddy glow emanated from a paper lantern above. The light hugged the contours of her hair, her delicately sloping shoulders, the soft arches of her breasts, smooth stomach, limber thighs, dark domains unfamiliar to him. She slid her fingernails along the slope of his abdomen. He felt crisp. They eased together, descending hands voyaging. He felt whole, confident, peaceful. Where they touched was union, physical and spiritual for him. Man and woman as he had dreamed.

He carried her to the double bed.

"No promises," she whispered.

Chapter Four

Herb's father couldn't be awakened. Coincidently, he'd spent the night in the guest bedroom of the family home after the departure of friends and family who came to the traditional Rizer break-fast after Yom Kippur: Temple Emanu-El's Rabbi Kaplan; doctors and missus Dyan, Katz, Michaels, and Shendi who were long time friends and literati; Boris Levin, arts curator at Bass; Myra Rubenstein of Florida Council for the Fine Arts; local musicians, Kass, Miranda, and Brown; artistic director and actors, Aubrey Crane, Melany Dunn, and Alvonica McKinnon—the progressive friends, patrons, and practitioners of his parents' immersions in community and culture.

A call came from Venetian Island as he peddled an exercise bike. Minnie had tried to wake Sol several times this morning, but not to worry, he was up and around now. Although there was no argument last night, Sol wasn't talking to her today. Herb heard his father grumbling, "Don't worry the boy," in the background. On a phone put to his ear by Minnie, Sol told his son how much he enjoyed Thanksgiving last night. "Jeez! Dad." Herb's outburst got his old man to stammer a cover for Thanksgiving with *holiday we celebrated*. Sol's responses came out uncommonly drawn. Dressed and out of his place in Coral Gables, Herb arrived at his family home less than a half hour after the call and minutes before an ambulance escorted his father to emergency at Mt. Sinai Hospital. Minnie had waited to call because Sol insisted she was crazy. When he accused her of an affair with the gardener and fell into a chair with a glazed, unresponsive look, she decided he needed a ride from Eastern Ambulance Service. Because a hospital suggested mortality, exposed private vulnerability, handed out public humiliation, heralded shameful dependence, Minnie feared going with her son. He was too distracted to argue. After securing a private duty nurse, Herb arrived at the hospital where his dad lay comatose.

Herb had returned to Miami because his dad suffered from erratic drops in blood pressure and lapses of speech like mini strokes except the man never actually fainted or fell. He'd become zombie like, but it passed in perhaps a minute or two, and Sol was as cantankerous as ever. Extensive outpatient tests revealed nothing. Hospital stays were spurned. Dad's heart was good, his lungs, likewise. A brain scan revealed nothing. His arteries were clear. A bit of dementia, the doctor said, and the onset of adult diabetes. Sol poo pooed Dr. Feldstein's diagnosis as an attempt to run up a bill. The supposed dementia Herb believed was merely loss of hearing. Sol had always been a selective listener, and old age italicized it. Diabetes, however, ran in his father's family, but seemed unrelated to the spells which only occurred with loss of blood pressure. All in all, Sol'd gotten a good bill of health and the episodes became infrequent and short lived. Nothing like what Herb now witnessed.

Beside his dad's guard-railed, electronically equipped, and plastic-coated bed, his white, epoxy teeth with shiny pink gums, bathed in a cleansing mixture. Only the blue, kidney-shaped hospital-issue container seemed strange. The celery and beige room with a grapevine boarder at its crown smelled medicinal and rancid. Herb checked the wastebasket, hanging locker, and bathroom for overlooked food, medical refuse, vinegar, ammonia, or any soiled laundry causing the stench. Nothing lay under the bed either. In the night stand though, an overturned bottle of something vile had leaked and dried and been overlooked by cleaning staff. When he returned from delivering the drawer, its contents, and complaint to the nurses station, Herb became anxious as his old man wheezed and had strained breathing like that requiring a respirator. For a moment, an alarmed son took in the heart rate, blood pressure, and other vital signs vacillating within normal ranges on a video monitor. When the breathing returned to normal, Herb unruffled somewhat. Likely his dad's temporary condition would lift as it had this morning.

Sol changed his diet to the demands of his pre-diabetic system. He been alert and active since the diagnosis and even hoodwinked the doctor into thinking that his condition was managed by exercise and healthy eating. Had the old man lost control of his blood sugar? A friend, certainly not a doctor, told him sulphur pills helped, and Sol took them. He knew better than doctors what was good and until now kept his machinery going. There had been no sign of anything wrong health-wise unless both parents had kept quiet or neither recognized changes. Yet after a day of holy day fasting and dinner last night, something went awry.

His father's occasional grunt and fetal position typified a sleep familiar to Herb. Familiar meant normal. Normal meant good. Among observations offspring make in their formative years, a parent's sleeping position seemed unusable information until now. Yet it was etched in his memory. The hospital bed was different, but the tucked up position held on from less menacing times. Sol and Minnie slept in a bedroom playfully named Buckingham Palace—thus he and his brother called the master suite in their Venetian Island home. Whenever his dad curled into a favorite snoring pose, it was fetal and normal. With his knees under his chest and both hands under one cheek as in this hospital bed, Sol looked like a bygone workday had been satisfying. The difference in his sleep now was elusive. Would he have lay so peacefully if he knew then that his wife would leave him? Did he drive her away? Had he longed for her to come back as she inevitably did? The continual unpleasantness in the empty nest of the Rizer home was a secret except from Herb and his brother.

"Thirsty?" He wasn't sure if it was said or thought. Undulating of his dad's crusted lips was taken as a *yes*. Graying eyebrows moved to say *yes*. His father's pupils darting beneath eyelids said *yes*. Was it foolhardy to believe as Beth had said that thoughts converge and psychic energy transmits them between loved ones? Did unopened eyes necessarily hinder a long overdue chat between father and son? *Have I told you that I love you, Dad?* Herb soaked a cloth at the sink and moistened his father's lips. Relief from chapped lips and untellable thirst?

What if damp cloths healed as effectively as medical intervention? Would Sol awaken and say, *Thanks, son. I love you, too.* Once long ago in childhood's shower, a washcloth like the one held to his dad's lips, scrubbed Herb's back. Turning unexpectedly, his eyes caught his dad at gut level and the soapy cloth swiped his face. Herb looked up at his father's strong contour—power he revered. When the soap stung, he rubbed his eyes with the backs of soapy hands which made him cry when the burn was so bad that he couldn't see. Then strong arms raised him into the cooling spray, and a gentle palm wiped away the sting. That scene stayed beyond its immediate importance yet effected whom Herb gently scrubbed in the showers of his life. With the wet hospital cloth rinsed, Herb wiped his dad's face.

Rounding the bed and adjusting the levellours for more daylight, he decided not to move his dad to face the window. Brightness contained some healing qualities. Summer light, after all, lifted winter blahs. When an elderly woman entered the room, Herb almost castigated the private duty nurse for dawdling until he realized that his mother, after all, overcame her fear of medical dependency and the social negatives of a hospital visit. He also suspected hysteria. She couldn't stay long and likely told her chauffeur to wait in the circular drive at the front portico. At bedside, she patted one of Sol's arms which converged under the sleeper's sagging cheek. She rubbed nervously. "Oh God, he's undernourished? Fasted all day and ate almost nothing last night. Oh God, he looks pale."

For two people who destroyed each other, separation worked as a rejuvenation. Never wanting or thinking of divorce, they drew slowly back together for, what was it now, the fifth time. Minnie mostly escaped to a single haven, her sister in Brooklyn Heights, a vacation home in Hendersonville, the Whitney Hotel in New Orleans, and now squatter's rights at Venetian Island while Sol *shmoozed* around Miami with movers and shakers, socialized, gambled, lost himself in work, drank excessively on occasion, and lived with an old floozy from Ojus, a *b* drinker from Miami

Beach's gambling heyday. Yet Minnie never held his separation lust as two-faced, adulterous, treacherous, or the like—always cordial, always reserved, always defending him, always playing the devoted wife as if realizing the tough hoe dad had living with her. How they kept up social appearances during separations was a marvel.

Herb wasn't sure she loved Sol except as an air plant loves its branch, but he was positive Sol loved her, had always, would always. How many more long hiatuses remained for them? What drove dad from a separate world back to a contentious one with this woman who likely had the word *love* stuck in her throat? "I want to talk to his doctor," Herb blurted. "Will you stay until I get back?"

Her bird-like nod gave him an okay to leave. Outside, he hesitated to be sure his mother would remain composed. He saw her slip Sol's hand from under a cheek. She touched it to hers. Silent, almost imperceptible twitches of her shoulders and frail back sent chills through Herb. He assumed she wiped tears with the back of Sol's hand. "I got over your brother Abie, Sol," she whispered. "You always told me I'd love you and I do." She tried to hold back, to be strong, to be supportive, to be hopeful, to show restraint, to find reprieve, but she was alone with an unconscious man and that was dangerous. The gasps came despite her efforts. How many times on the brink had she bitten a lower lip, almost drawing blood, to stave off an emotional flood. The expected, though, ended in a reversal as she plaintively said, "Please. Sing to me, Sollie."

Dr. Feldstein was nowhere to be found. The duty nurse sent Herb to the *B* wing as she believed the internist had returned to his office. Not so, the secretary informed him. The doctor might be lunching in the cafeteria and, unless an emergency existed, he could not be accessible without a page. Herb's dad lying comatose in a critical care bed, breathing erratically, subjected to foul odors, unattended and unable to ask for help did not constitute an emergency? What the hell state of affairs required immediate attention then? The secretary went on rather pointedly to say that the doctor would do rounds after lunch. The waiting room served as a good place to await a prognosis. Doctors need down time undisturbed, she loyally preached. Wending back to the room, Feldstein's name came through loud and clear on the public address system and the flashing lights in the corridor confirmed that someone else's emergency took the medic's valuable lunch time.

It seemed logical that intervention ought come prior to crisis. With all conceivable tests, monitors, drugs, interventions, precautions, a human being should be safe in this hospital environment. If life neared conclusion, the crisis should be discussed with family beforehand. Upon his return to critical care, Herb was escorted by a duty nurse to a green waiting room, and she insisted that he might best serve the situation by calming his mother while Dr. Feldstein worked on Mr. Rizer Senior. He barely sat beside Minnie when the crestfallen MD stood before them shaking his head sadly as if his pet Basset had just been put down. The doctor issued a standard, medical school phrase like, "We did all we could to save him."

There wasn't much to do for Minnie who repeated at each opportunity, "Go in to him. He'd want that." A hug met with, "Go in to him." Half sentences were interrupted with, "Go in to him." A suggestion that she come along got her arms snugly crisscrossed, "Go in to him." So the dutiful son did as told. The old man lay on the bed. His breathing stopped, furor of life's last moments had passed, the frenzy of the nurses and doctor dissipated to another part of the hospital. It was quiet. Herb stood bedside. False teeth still bathed in the kidney container. The drawer hadn't been replaced in the night stand. Levellours opened to daylight which continued to pour onto the mechanical bed with plastic accouterments. The monitor screen said nothing Herb didn't already know. A damp washcloth lay neatly folded beside the sink. His mother sat in the waiting room. An on-duty social worker entered. "We'll meet in the waiting room. Is your mother there?"

"I'll come in a minute. Close the door, please."

The old man lay on his back half covered by a disheveled blanket. He was bare from the waist up. Newborns were as helplessly pale as his father. Herb reached under the body and lifted. A revered head flopped loosely back; once brisk, caring hands hung limply on the rumpled sheet. The man felt tepid. Herb palmed his father's head onto one shoulder and encompassed the body like a new born in a parent's arms rocking back and forth. He sang, "Heavenly shades of night are falling, it's twilight time . . . ."

Chapter Five

Herb rode with his older brother, sister-in-law, and mom in a Mercedes limo down a mahogany lined street toward the cemetery. Verdant, almost iridescent, leaf canopies surrounded massive, black-furrowed trunks like weathered coffins beneath a caretaker's hedge. The rabbi who faced the mourners spoke of Billy Cyprus's tribute to Sol. In all his years, the clergyman witnessed no one who commanded such respect from the Seminole community. And the deaf mute, what was the name, ah yes, Victor Ashton—a childhood story, one about your dad's good works, a story of a boy's righteousness in the Jewish tradition—both eulogies praised a soul filled with *tsdokeh* and *mitsveh*. A dad's empty pine box rode in the hearse. Sol Rizer's ashes, boxed in cardboard and brown wrapping, rested in Max Alvarez's trunk. The cremation, the wish of the deceased, had been rejected for burial. Jewish law and custom be damned. Honor a good man's request. Yet Sol's ashes interred beside other departed family members remained on hold.

The overcast sky shed grays across yards of houses on each side of the street. A coral-rock wall with wrought-iron gate marked the conservative Jewish burial ground. Above the gate read, "Star of David," and Herb imagined its subtitle, "Where Cremation is Sacrilege." A flower vendor waved at the passing entourage of headlighted vehicles.

Inside the soaring gate, the road narrowed. Flowers in permanent vases spotted the cemetery. Neatly clipped hedges separated sections of Miami's Jewish ancestry, and a dozen or so live oak trees, almost a century old, spotted the drive. Homes to roadside became rows of noted family plots—Hirshmeyer, Wolfson, Stone, Aronowitz, Weiss, Singer, Novak, Mufson, Cohen—lavish headstones, granite and alabaster mausoleums, and marble slabs with bronze nameplates that looked like stepping stones to an unseen mansion. The line of vehicles ran the length of the cemetery and then some. Minnie removed a few old bar mitzvah yarmulkas from a velour pouch as if they had been saved in anticipation of this funeral. She placed one next to Herb and Jake and stepped from the limo almost before it stopped as if not to wait in line for a husband's burial. Walking beside her and ahead of everyone else, Herb passed Gurber, Janowitz, Melkin, and other graves lining the path to a canopy where an ample crowd, most of the throng from the synagogue service, would soon assemble. Now standing above the vault, he imagined a vacant space filled with cold, black mold which grew up its sides; in its center, a rotting, empty pine box. He could not comprehend the end of anyone, let alone his dad.

The night following his father's death, Herb shared with Beth the cremation and funeral plans. Perhaps talking of death and burial might jolt his senses. Not one tear coursed his cheek nor one sigh moved his lips. An intellectual halo surrounded his grief with details of cremation, last wishes, coordinating tasks with his brother, notifying family and friends, sorting through personal items, tending to Minnie, arranging *shiveh*, monitoring business, making funeral arrangements, and such. As they lay nude in Beth's bed, unsought sympathy came as love making, particularly intense, as if loss drifted toward their horizon like a setting sun. In Beth's arms, love overpowered grief, gain eclipsed loss, death became life, negatives became positives. As she lay in the crook of his arm, the world seemed kind, sadness appeared anachronous, endings looked like beginnings. Small matter if she loathed funerals and asked that he come back to her when the grotesque rituals of grief ended. "How long will your mourning last," she asked? "How many days will you pine for his return? Till then, lover boy, sensual memory will need to suffice for me."

She more than he drew them together. Was her need greater? Wasn't she the professor of love? He the pupil? But as sunsets came and went, he wished to spend nights in her company. Perhaps a father's death hadn't any room in a son's overwhelming desire, his gluttonous passion, separation angst, overanxious presence, guilt for wanting to

24

transgress propriety and tell the world how he felt, tell Max Alvarez, Miss Ferringer, Dr. Beaumont, in fact, all of the university from whom the affair remained secret. Sworn to silence as if his love, his attention, his presence threatened a reputation she guarded fiercely, he felt so temporary. He didn't care what the world said. He felt no shame for honest adoration. He felt stronger than censure, job loss, ostracism, finding Ferringer's line of impropriety to cross. Yet fear kept him from saying, "I love you," but when he finally did, fear and doubt came as unwanted side effects. *I love you* was a heavy commitment that could not be withdrawn without grave aftermath and emotional forfeiture. An admission of love lassoed one's heart and soul where Helen of Troy, centuries earlier, tied a lover to inevitability. If Beth walked out like Mary, there'd be little left of him to piece back together. *All the king's horses and all the king's men. . . .*

As planned, Herb couldn't get Sol's ashes from Max Alvarez's trunk into the casket which now sat on ropes and pulleys above a deep, dark hole in the earth. The rabbi and funeral staff acted like guardians as if they expected the ashes to be placed in the coffin. Rabbi Kaplan just finished *Kaddish* and Herb and the others used phonetic transliterations to chant along with the prayer for the dead, "Yis-gad-dal v'yes-kad-dash sh'may rab'bo . . . ." After the twenty-third psalm, each of the Rizers took a handful of dirt from a silver tray brought by a congregant who leaned down to Minnie, kissed her cheek, and passed a note that defiantly ignored customary burial rites. Minnie went to the tomb and let the earth fall slowly from her hand onto the coffin. Once again Herb saw her frail back twitch and shoulders raise slightly, yet in the silence of the occasion, not a whimper came. Again he felt shivers: not for his loss but for hers. She appeared frozen in time like her husband, her lover, friend, soul mate with whom fifty-odd years presented interesting and tumultuous times that her partner's hidden memoir, his secret diary, his lifelong journal would recount. Then reminded of the crushed note in hand, she opened it as if to read a final goodbye from a well-wisher. The ominous, hateful thing took her breath away. Her knees buckled, and she might have fallen face first and headlong onto the tomb had Herb not caught her in mid swoon. He held his mother in his arms while Jake and Jenny tossed their dirt on the coffin as the rabbi had directed, and the empty coffin was lowered into its final resting place. His brother snatched the note from the ground and they strode off, Minnie unconscious in Herb's arms. Folks in the back of the gathering had no idea what happened and people in front deferred to Herb's control, the family's decisive action, and the rabbi's request to remain calm. The rabbi led a final prayer which faded as the distance between the service and the family widened.

In the limo, smelling salts revived Minnie, and Herb read the hand written note dropped beside his father's tomb. It read, *Your blaspheming husband's ashes will never rest beneath consecrated earth in a Jewish cemetery. May his soul wander for eternity.* The yellow piece of notepad paper bore no signature, no coward's name to credit its malefactor, no meddler to face, no offender to strike back at, no religionist to harass, no envious ogre to vilify. It confirmed Herb's feeling that some men take religion away from God, that conservative institutions often harbor vengeful practitioners, yet that men of faith remain God's workman. Sol Rizer's ashes would be buried at the grave site as he requested even if his younger son had to sneak in under cloak of midnight with a pick and shovel and do it himself.

Chapter Six

Freshmen Composition came in twos—two hour blocks, twice a week, two classes, double work. The challenge for Herb was boosting unprepared freshmen to meet college standards before they were axed. Bowman F. Ashe denied no one higher education as long as he or she maintained average grades. Especially challenging were athletes whose claim to academics was tossing or catching a ball. Beth offered no suggestions, but commiserated with the daunting task of rehabilitation within the confines of an impossible time frame. She told him that Freshman Composition was the hell hole of the department. Doctorates and research faculty failed miserably at teaching it while blaming everyone and everything but themselves. They flunked over sixty percent of remedial freshmen and forced research assistants or graduate students to teach the motley brood. The athletic director had continual grade patrol for players.

The semester began with, "Write the story of your family's relocation to Miami." When Herb read the student work, he was floored. What had public schools done to native speakers of the English language? A student from the Congo and one from France, newcomers to the language for God's sake, were the only understandable writers in the class. The worst of the narratives barely spelled *Miami* correctly and the best found ends of sentences with punctuation other than commas or dashes.

First off, Herb sent his students to the language lab with permission from a Spanish prof to record their compositions and bring the tape to class with hard copies to pass around. In his view, listening to an essay and seeing your faulty written structure raised flags and caused one to think about the process of communication. Listening to one's own essay on a recording seemed an excellent jump start. The papers contained too many language fractures to begin with the teaching of traditional grammar. And students were too smart and out of time for a rearview mirror, basic-skills approach. Teaching writing to the American masses paralleled teaching English as a second language. Using a volunteer's composition, each class worked on linguistic tools—simple syntax, meaning, punctuation, spelling, word order, reducing or removing irrelevant material, focusing on subject, revising, revising, revising—to make their written communication readably realistic. His classes worked in groups with one benchmark—would you understand this phrase, sentence, paragraph if the author (he used the word loosely) were not here to explain? The best part of a month the freshmen analyzed and revised a first and only assigned composition. They came for office consultations whenever class wasn't sufficient, and by the next assignmen—explain your position on rioting for social change—he witnessed ample growth in clarity and form and some proud kids who chose to submit typewritten work instead of hand-scrawled papers. Their second essay needed considerably less revision.

Shortly after the use of the language lab, he was called before the throne of Lola May Ferringer, Vice President for Personnel. "Several of your colleagues brought to my attention, Mr. Rizer, that your freshmen overloaded the foreign language laboratory with an assignment approved by you. Is my information correct, sir?"

"I believe so."

"The facility in question is reserved for foreign language students."

"Likely, I'm misinterpreting the meaning of language as clearly within my discipline."

"I'm sure I don't know to what you refer, sir."

"My students bought tapes, and my assignment cost the university not a penny beyond its budget."

"The equipment belongs to the foreign language department."

"I asked permission."

"The point is, Mr. Rizer, English instructors stay within certain boundaries. Your department has tape recorders, overhead projectors, film and video equipment—is that not so?"

"The lab was the only way to overcome time restraints."

"Hereafter, you will refrain from overstepping organizational decorum."

"The growth my kids achieved was educationally sound."

"Did you assign a paper on race riots?"

"Is my academic freedom in question as well?"

"Kent State infected quite enough of academia and the arts, thank you. In these times, we keep careful watch on agitators."

"I'll keep my eyes open, too."

"Traditional boundaries must be observed. Do I make myself clear, mister?"

"Didn't Boman F. Ashe preach educational opportunity?"

"Thank you for that bit of information and for coming, Mr. Rizer. This time, close the door on your way out."

One of the relocation essays caught Herb's attention. The young man was one receiving a tuition waiver for modern dance. Not only was the essay nearly illegible, but almost unintelligible. *Me and mine come here from Moultrie and tooken care of cause I be the oldest wilest my mama and pap goes long weekends out a drinking. I tooken milk out Piggly Wiggley and stale bread and old stuff they's a dumping from the white folks clinic down on Chalmers. Wednesday he come home to wallop cause they tied one on at Gene and Rens Juke Joint down around Jessup. Sissy queer he call my name and use back of his hand side my head. The law she say come here with the baby shook to pieces. He stop some but mama be bloodied up and all bruise face. Pap passing out and we got his old ford stole and away with some clothes and jar money. Drive Alvin she say with them all sleeping in the flatbed to her sister in Liberty City. That's how we nine come to Miami. Me driving the little ones to Dunbar and myself and I to Allapatah.*

The language lab exercise helped Alvin McKinnon

considerably. For one, he was highly motivated to overcome his honors English background from an inner city school which, if it stressed nothing else, taught him that adopting white-speak meant turning one's back on black-speak, honky speak meant rejecting his brothers and his culture, *The Man* speak meant slighting his roots. His honors class did little more than work on projects like collages, reports, socio-dramas, memorization, but did little reading and less writing. Being now in a WASP-ish environment, Alvin realized that Ma Bell would never go for, *oh, fo, fo, fo, ny-en,* and that Herb's curriculum seemed a fast track to standard English for Liberty City inbreeds. He became a voracious re-writer and usurper of Herb's office hours and after office hours, but Alvin as a teaching project was intriguing for the boy seemed to be giving Herb a crash course in how to present writing concepts powerfully and effectively. He tapped into Alvin's interest in drama and had him memorize and recite dialect: passages from Bernard Shaw, Tennessee Williams, Brecht, Ibsen, O'Neil, and others then write short, spinoff pieces of his own using an actor's ear for diction. It became common to get a call at the office or at home and hear, "Let me say at the outset that my name is James Clarence Withencroft . . . ," in Oxford dialect. Alvin became particularly adept at cockney, a Southern drawl, Midwest Standard, and New York gangster. His spinoffs were imaginative and engrossing, and the kid caught *word fever*. Herb got quite a kick out of him when returning from a Booker T. and Hialeah football game. Alvin mimicked a Miami accent in a piece comparing the violence of the Roman Colosseum to a football stadium. His homework had appropriate spelling, punctuation, and structure except for the cheering crowd, *Hawya-leeya, Hawya-leeya.*

Since Alvin's dance debut was a campus function, Herb and Beth happened upon each other accidentally on purpose at the Ring Theater. They saw the boy dance and sing the role of Bernardo in a production of *West Side Story.* At the outset, Alvin took command of the Sharks and of an audience that rose to its feet spontaneously at his curtain call.

Shortly thereafter, Beth painted an expressionistic oil on canvass—the same angular, grotesque woman as on the walls of her Grove apartment with a gazelle-like dancer soaring in a *grand jete* at the viewer and above the audience. The smoothness of his skin and stark, primary slashes of colors highlighting his street clothes contrasted with the muted, rough texture of the drab artist. She gave the painting to Herb who brought it to class and asked the freshmen to write about it. The assignment inspired new heights in their composition careers, yet Herb believed that Alvin was the only one who recognized the subject of the painting. He approached the podium after class and began, "Ain't no one never—" Herb looked up from marking a thesaurus. "Double negative?" the boy asked. Herb nodded. "Mr. Rizer, sir, nobody in all my years done a jive thing–" he pointed at the painting and smiled as if having found the meaning of art appreciation, "—a respectful thing like that for me till today."

"Call me Herb."

"Pardon if I ask?"

"Go on."

"You need some help around the office?"

"If I do, I'll ask. Thanks."

"How about, you know, around your place and such."

"That's generous. I'm here at school mostly. But thank's anyway."

"You ever ate souse?"

"Don't know what that is, Alvin."

"I can bring you some?"

"Thank you."

"One day soon, Mr. Herb, I'll get hold of a way to say thanks." Alvin backed away looking at the floor until he was out of the room and of Herb's line of sight. But the kid didn't quit with souse which turned out to be the most vile dish offered to liberal Jewish tastebuds. He'd show up at the office to do filing or organizing—done quite well. Surprisingly, the kid stuck his head in without knocking at Herb's apartment in the Gables for work duty. Did he look in through Herb's always unlocked door on other occasions?

Eyeball to eyeball, Herb explained the nature of privacy which Alvin hardly understood what with brothers, sisters, aunt, and mom—ten in all—living in a two bedroom place. A course of study did not require duty or payback from students since the university paid for a teacher's efforts. When he got to the awkward visit, the boy asked if he might walk Winnie, Herb's Collie, whenever the boss man wasn't able to do it himself.

"Try to see how inappropriate this is from my point of view."

"Please, Mr. Herb."

"We should go back to Mr. Rizer and Mr. McKinnon."

"There's carryings on in my mind because of what you done for me."

"What do you mean?"

"God, I wish I knowed?"

"Look, Mr. McKinnon, I can't use you in my office or at home."

"Cause I'm black?"

"Oh, God."

"I won't bother you none. Tell me when you ain't home, and I'll let myself in and walk the dog for you."

"If I say 'no'?"

"They's other ways to payback."

"Likely you have Greek ancestors."

"African, I mostly guess."

"Agreed. Now go home."

"You won't never regret this, Mr. Herb. Thank you."

Whenever returning home thereafter, he found Winnie fed, the dishes washed and dried, the place organized and cleaned. Beth armchair-analyzed the boy as needing a father figure in his life. Herb might have accepted that premise if he wasn't closer in age to being Alvin's brother. What he failed to connect was a certain prominent local actress, a woman his father patronized, an artist who, for years, came to the annual Rizer Yom Kippur break fast, an artist whose break in show business Sol arranged. He had nurtured and polished her raw talent. Alvonica McKinnon, displaced mother of eight, refugee from Moultrie, Georgia, resident of Liberty City, Bess of *Porgy and Bess,* mama in Hellman's *A Raisin in the Sun*, lead in *Ma Rainey's Black Bottom*, was Alvin McKinnon's mama.

Chapter Seven

Glistening, azure water in a pool refracted sunlight as if secrets lay below its surface. A two-story gingerbread ornamented motel with a galvanized steel roof and glass jalousies overlooked a gentle Atlantic as palm fronds fingered the glass windows to touch whatever lay inside. White and brown-strapped lounge chairs—some with floral cushions—were scattered about the deck, all empty but for one. An occasional gaudy towel sat on a foot rest or seat to save places for crowded-city-minded tourists. A natural blond in a heliotrope bikini set a straw hat on the deck and rolled a pelican towel under her neck. She had a smear of white zinc under each eye. Her aloneness was the epitome of privacy among a sea of tropical furniture. Her oiled body blended into the bleached, limestone deck and faded pink of a knee-high perimeter wall. No redness appeared on her alabaster figure. She looked Grecian, goddess-like, except for the beginnings of crow's feet which she covered with the woven straw hat.

A youth coming from the turquoise ocean smoothed his chestnut hair back. He wiped brine from his pockmarked face and crossed the limestone to a chaise next to the blond. Working toward but not yet achieving a swimmer's body, he was hairless, masculinely symmetrical, close to firm from a regimen on an exercise bike, and tanned. He sat beside her. Water dripped from his finger onto her stomach and wet her navel. He then drew rings around it. She laughed. When she playfully tried to pull her hat back in place, he tossed it on an adjacent chair. Finding not a soul present, he slid his palms over her alabaster flesh then kissed her passionately, longingly and slipped his hand below the cinch of her bikini. Her hips raised slightly to greet him.

She snuck her hand below the drawstring of his navy swimsuit. Did they believe the motel void of guests, a life guard, a manager, gardener? Moving together as though a cocoon spun secrecy around love's gestures, they fell into an embrace concealed by voyeur-less windows. If a tourist came upon them, he'd be a stranger anyway. The few they'd met so far had been. As lovers lost in self-indulgence often did, they ignored propriety and used the pool, its deck, the beach, the bar—everything out of hearing or seeing distance of an intruder. Why flaunt publically what each had known privately in a room the night before and the night before that? Was it the *caw* of a seagull, the rustle of branches against the building, or Herb's arousal that caused him to draw slowly away? She removed her palm from his suit. Both her cheeks had reddened as well as spots around her neck. Telltales of excitement reshaped her halter top. She fixed her bikini so that it appeared undisturbed. Drops of perspiration formed above her blue eyes which were dabbed with the pelican towel so as not to smear the zinc. "I dreamt you rescued me from an island where I was being sacrificed to the native god of love," she whispered into his ear and fondled the lobe of it between her teeth.

After fixing his own swim trunks, Herb helped her up. The straw hat covered an aroused extremity of his heart. He felt like a teen with an after-class book front and center. At the door which he held, Beth cased the lobby for judgmental eyes. They were checked in as husband and wife, and Herb didn't care who speculated otherwise. That they were together mattered most. But she acted skittish and that, in his estimation, cast doubt on their ploy. An old couple stood at check-in reading tourist brochures. When the unoiled hinges squeaked, the woman turned. She reset a white bow on her terrycloth beach robe, and her brown Kino sandals clacked on the cream Marvel tiles as she left her companion at the counter. "Beth Shockett, dear, is it such a small world? I just waved *hello* to Dr. Shockett at the Duval Gallery. Dear man recommended the Crazy Conch but said nothing of staying at this motel. He's such a private sort, I imagine. Aren't the rooms quaint?"

Beth wrapped a pelican beach towel around her midriff. "Miss Ferringer? Marvin didn't tell me he saw you. We'd have sent up a complimentary basket of fruit for you and your—uh—friend. You are staying together?" She eyed the old gentleman while the matron watched Herb grapple with the hat as he came in.

"Is that Mr. Rizer a guest here?" she whispered.

Silence extended beyond normal courtesy. "I guess." Beth grinned. "We ran into each other at the pool," she said. "He's here with a girlfriend." As Herb approached, she added, "And now, Miss Ferringer, I meet you and your beau, c'est la vie. The university seems to favor Key West."

Lola May eyed the hat obscuring Herb's privates. As prurient spinsters were prone to speculation, Lola May glared. Herb wanted to drop the hat and let her see his bulge, but decided against it—moral impropriety and all that crap. Yet her sardonic grin gave the impression she already guessed why he held a hat over his groin. She said laughingly, "If any more UM'ers pop up, we can have a real party," and turned her back on him.

Lola May's old companion shuffled toward the impromptu soiree as if he expected an honest introduction. He was a man who moved by leaning his body in the desired direction. His beige Bermuda shorts were too ready-to-wear for a man with a thick waist and spindly legs which was why he wore suspenders and a belt. And the tropical bird shirt with parrots, flamingos, and herons was beyond garish for a Floridian. Its cobalt background clashed with his canary yellow, panama hat. Seeing Beth wrapped in a towel brought a lascivious smile to his lips which disappeared when he eyed Herb.

Lola May Ferringer took his cue. "This is Barry Whorton, a cousin of mine from Eustis. Meet Beth Shockett. She's with the English department. Her husband, the doctor we met at the gallery, is head of neurology at the university hospital. They're checked in here." The old man smiled. After pecking Beth's hand, he extended his to Herb who stepped between the two women. The men shook hands. "And who have we here, young man?"

"Herb Rizer," he said. "English department, also."

"Weren't you at Hunter College?" Barry asked.

"Assistant registrar. You're psychology, right?"

"Retired," the old man offered.

"To the pleasures of Eustis?" Herb asked.

"Figuratively speaking." The old man grinned furtively.

Herb went on dauntlessly, "How does—let me see if I recall—your wife Rebecca—right—like Florida."

Barry's smile disappeared. "Remind me of other things we had at Hunter. My ex wife and I are in training for second-time-around dating."

Miss Ferringer looked at the floor. "My—I mean, coincidentally, of course, it is a small world as they say in Disneyland that you two men should have history together. Barry is such a kidder. His wife, Florence, is in their room." She chortled into her cleavage as if her joke might relax a revival of religious fundamentalists. Then furrows set in at her brow as she glanced at his hat covered boner. For her take on the matter, Herb need only count the myriad Grecian sculptures at the Vatican with penises broken off. But what the hell, this wasn't campus; the viper had no jurisdiction; private lives were just that, private. And surely the moral propriety line employees were not to breach had ironic duality in the lobby of the Crazy Conch. Herb doubted anyone, particularly Lola May Ferringer, would throw the first stone. However, one positive aspect of meeting the vice president at a remote motel in the Keys—it quickly negated the need for a woman's straw hat to get through the lobby. So on to his head it went.

Beth fiddled with the tuck holding the pelican beach towel in place. "We must get together, Miss Ferringer, while you're here."

Perhaps the new-found affair gave Lola May empowerment. Whorton would probably go along with her cousin rouse. But in a short time, the old battleaxe would ferret out that Beth and Herb were staying together. Lola May relaxed and adopted a righteous tone. "Your husband probably rented the best room in this place for you, dearie? Am I right?"

Beth came back so quickly that *am I right* almost got stepped on. Her beautiful voice was firm but hushed. "You introduced Cousin Barry to me in Mt. Dora and Avon Park. Did you forget? Our paths seem destined to cross, Miss Ferringer. I trust you're having fun together on these family rendezvous?"

"Well," said Barry Whorton, "I'd certainly remember meeting a lady pretty as you, my dear, if I weren't at an age where memory fails me."

Ferringer drew her collar tight and raised her chin. Her voice had that official aloofness Herb recognized from office visits. "I would hope we'd have more fun than you two. We have so much less time and energy than the young, I assure you, Mrs. Shockett."

Beth shifted her weight from one foot to the other. Hers was the move film makers liked for foreshadowing eminent hair-pulling, scratching, biting, and clothes-tearing that came with a girly-fight. "Herb, be a dear," Beth said. "My sunglasses are by the pool." Herb walked out. Someone, although there was still no one around the pool, must have taken off with them. He checked the path back in case they had fallen out of her rolled up towel. Nothing. When he returned, Lola May and her friend were gone. Beth'd used the hat on his head to cover her eyes, she remembered, and the glasses were probably on the dresser in the room.

"You acted like you didn't know me," Herb said.

"Herb, be reasonable. If I knew she came here—"

"We're off campus, for God's sake."

"The woman is a vindictive watchdog and a morals barometer for Florida."

"We didn't care who knew about us, remember?"

"A female can lose her job like that." She snapped her fingers.

"I'd take care of you." He moved her toward the stairs, and she looked around like a mouse in a place with cats. Arm around her waist, he escorted her toward their room. "Who's this doc, the old battleaxe mentioned?"

"My ex."

"Who's the Whorton guy?"

"Lola May's off-campus lover." At the top of the stairs, she asked him to let her go into the room and to please be sure the hall was clear before following. Upon opening the door, he found her on the double bed lying on her pelican beach towel. She looked like sunshine, so radiant, iridescent, and perfect for any man fortunate enough to receive her charm and affection. Yet he sensed that Lola May Ferringer dampened what he'd felt since checking in days ago—carefree abandon, anonymity, rapture. The pretense of campus life hung in the air as if the motel were the English office, and the room was a retreat from judgment. He closed the Venetian blinds. "What's wrong," he said sitting at the edge of the bed.

She curled around him. "Not a thing."

He ran his fingers through her hair.

The response lay somewhere between neutral and warm. She said, "Ask yourself what's wrong."

"Why?"

She rubbed his tummy. "My face can't be as long as yours."

"Thought it was. I'm smiling. See. Ferringer wants to know what we have together. Love needs challenge. Why are you afraid?"

Like sunshine shaded by blinds, her light faded in the dim atmosphere of a bed whereupon both had witnessed social immunity. She began, "I thought I was ready. Being alone becomes too comfortable after a time. I've lost the confidence and security taken for granted when I was married to Melvin. Divorce takes time to fade. Hurt takes time. Please don't let this end because of my hangups."

Without reservation, hesitation, or conceit, his answer came like a reflex, "I can't think of endings. I've gone farther than I ever imagined."

"Is that a good thing?"

"I don't know."

"You've made me feel whole again and so happy with you. What's changed?"

"Why pretend? We're no longer casual acquaintances. Why be cagy? We're here together and in love. Why lie? A divorce shouldn't be secret." He kissed her. "I love you enough to be hurt."

She slipped her hand into the back of his bathing suit and let her hand roam. "I'm yours, lover. For now, don't doubt me." She rested her cheek on his shoulder. "I'm your Lisa and you're my David. Tell me the time, and I'll make a rhyme." She giggled. "If we play out *The Sound and The Fury*. I'm Caddy and you're my, Dalton Ames. But don't expect a child from me, illegitimate or otherwise."

There, in the open, was a bite he hadn't counted on. The surprise made him grate like a sailboat hull against rock. He craved her scent, warmth, delicacy but focused on some obscure doctor visiting a gallery in Key West where an old bitch found superiority in what she thought she knew. Fear rolled across land's end where his body and mind were aground. Was it a shore where her *ex* waited to wreck them amid love's wondrous journey? "Don't explain the child comment," he said.

"How can I not? When our minds superimposed, I felt your need for family."

"Leave *us* in nirvana."

"Family is not a part of my future."

"So not a part of mine then." Hadn't family always been in his makeup? Weren't kids a social norm? Yes, she sensed his desire to live a life with her, to propose marriage which occupied his thoughts. Yet he'd respected her wounds. *No promises,* ground rules set at the beginning of Herb and Beth; set by her, observed by him. Yet *please don't use me* was her barometer of mutual trust.

"I can't bare any more kids," she said.

He stood. Her hand dropped from his swimsuit. He looked at the fan turning on the ceiling, tallied water stains in the plaster. "What do you mean MORE?" He watched her turn on the bed, place her right hand under her cheek, her back to him.

Flatly she said, "Our daughter lives with my ex."

Herb could not understand how after several nights together, he had overlooked broken plaster above the headboard, a few ends of the Venetians broken off, a greyish stain on the lavender bedspread. What child did he believe the subject of her oils to be? Didn't he mistake photos in her apartment to be a niece, a sister, a distant cousin? What storehouse of wedges could life drive between lovers? He said nothing because the last to speak might hurt the other by redefining an unblemished weekend and the prerequisite lovemaking that led to it. Couldn't she see in his soul the *us* he worshiped?

She sat up on the bed. "I watched you in the classroom. It's clear that you love kids."

"Your opening line for a parting scene is overwritten."

"That's a mean thing to say. My *ex* has that streak. Is it indigenous to the gender?"

"Oh, God. Forgive me."

Like two ships passing silently in the night, they fixed on running lights to avoid collision. Was she driving a wedge between them because Ferringer checked into the motel? If Herb found a room elsewhere, would Beth lay off kids in their future or Mary in his past? The riff seemed out of proportion, especially for him because he had the most to lose by coming into virility with his true soul mate. Beth was hot. And he had the hots—incurable hots. How one unhinged from them was beyond reason and emotion. It was the stuff tragedies were made of.

She spoke first. "I couldn't bear resentment."

He kept in check the boiling emotional stew below the surface as best as possible. He sat next to her on the bed. "I can rethink my God damn values—over twenty-one, you know." He placed her palm on his heart. "Do you feel that?" he asked.

"Ever since we met."

"Don't try to rescue it."

She moved away and pulled the Venetian blinds up. The sudden light shocked him. The cord slipped from her grasp and they crashed down like a child falling. Beth jumped back and yelped. Once again the room was in shadows. Now headed directly for his running lights, she stopped dead in the water. "I won't bare another child."

Before weighing the corrosiveness of his words, they came. "Can't or won't, which is it?"

And she sounded ready for the collision. "For me, one and the same."

Chapter Eight

Cantilevered over the Gulf of Mexico, the Key Wester Restaurant contained more Dade County Pine from its pilings to rafters than most historic structures on the island. Built before the Hurricane of twenty-eight which destroyed Flagler's railroad, the rough pine came to the Southern most city in regular freight shipments from the East Coast Railway Terminal in downtown Miami. Termite resistant, the wood was a popular building material up to and through the second World War. The pine built restaurant tonight was almost empty although Florida lobsters still crawled backwards in a lobby aquarium. The cashier who normally kept busy at the register filled sugar jars at the side stand. Tiki torches spread a romantic ambiance around waterside tables. Their flames reflected like swarms of fireflies on rippling brine below. Silhouettes of jack, tarpon, and barracuda slunk beneath the water's surface awaiting scraps that patrons tossed over routinely. A pre-teen leaned over the rail and got the surface boiling with struggling jack unwilling to share tidbits. A barracuda scattered them. Tarpon broke the surface whether or not they were fed.

A lanky waiter swished his way past cypress tables to one waterside place where he mixed a Caesar salad in front of a couple sipping conch chowder from Fiesta ware. The salads served, he held a pepper mill awaiting a nod. Then he raised a bottle of Sherry to indicate that the soup might be greatly improved with a slosh for most tourists didn't know the sweet wine was to enhance the chowder. Herb shook his head and Beth placed her palm above the bowl of chowder. The waiter smiled and set the Sherry on his tray. "I've been admiring that ring, hon. Its fabulous. Family heirloom?"

Beth held out her hand. "My ex gave it to me."

"You her ex, Bruce?"

Herb shook his head and noticed that she wore the thing on her ring finger. She never wore jewelry. Why hadn't he noticed it?

"I wish my mate had your ex's taste, darling." The waiter flapped his hand. "Be back with your entrees, ma'am," he said and left as lightly as he'd arrived.

Beth played with the salad. "I'm going home tonight. You can stay or go. Please yourself."

"We were driving back day after tomorrow, I thought."

"I think not."

"Who'll take you back? If you insist, I will, of course."

"I need to be alone."

"On a Greyhound bus, for God's sake, or only away from me?"

"I don't want to answer that question."

Herb felt a thwack inside his chest like a machete slicing tree pulp. His words came slow, deliberate, like mind grating body. "You're going back with Melvin Shockett, aren't you?"

"We're at the turning point. There are reasons for changes that are best kept unspoken until the conclusion."

"Is this a play? Life spiced with dramatic irony. A denouement re-written to change the outcome?"

"Please don't be angry. We'll always be together—always. I love you."

"Why am I thinking you mean metaphorically?"

"I'm your Lisa, your Caddy. For a brief time we saw the eyes of God. Now there's a price to pay."

"So you're going home with the mystery man old Ferringer thinks followed you here. This doesn't make sense."

"No promises, remember?"

"You led me beyond that. Promises got out unwillingly. I vowed honest love. Can you honor that vow?"

"We both came willingly."

"Come back to the motel with me now."

"Please, Herb."

"What's happened?" He wanted tears, he expected tears, but her cheeks were dry. Hadn't they laughed together, loved together as if one heart served two bodies? He felt her

44

rhythm as deeply as his own. He damned the man who drew her away. Did she need to be hurt again by the very man who broke her? Herb needed a Manhattan. After the first hefty swig, he wanted to say *fuck off*, go home with Shockett and let him beat the emotional shit out of you, but the *I don't care* part clogged his throat, and Herb's heart wouldn't allow his lips that free fall. When he raised the glass again it was nearly empty. This exit had to be because of his insensitivity, he told himself. He raced through a myriad of indiscretions but flagged none as a catalyst. Yet differences need time to erode love's alabaster finish. This scene lacked rationality.

Parting suddenly was unnatural. Hadn't it taken Mary two weeks to send him home from Minnesota. And afterward, whenever he called wasn't her ear as sympathetic as his ear was to her? She was ruled by parents who crippled her and buried the relationship. Beth had no such intervention. Hadn't he honored the taboos set by her? If being with Beth meant no family, so it would be. Why wouldn't she believe him? "What have I done? I'd apologize if I understood."

She gazed at her salad. Her hands tugged and clawed at her abdomen as if to relieve pain. The vigorous ritual caught the attention of a family several tables behind Beth. She whispered raspingly, "The bastard left me in delivery all alone." She sobbed now. Herb envisioned a delivery room where she lay in childbirth without assistance. She spread her legs and panted. He took her hands from their task which seemed to draw her back from memory. The clawing of her midriff left snags on her dress. She breathed irregularly as if there were some physical strain to be resolved. Rubbing her arm calmed her. She moved his hand to her cheek. "I can't marry you."

The table candle flickered. Water rippled as a tarpon turned the surface. She'd returned from some hospital room to the cypress table on a cantilevered deck above the Gulf of Mexico in the Key Wester Restaurant and an untouched salad which she moved aside as she leaned toward him. Tears at the edges of her blue eyes glistened in candlelight, and he saw into her soul. Yes, there was love, but to whom did it belong—not to him, not to Shockett, not to anyone. It had the fury of his own love but the wrong object. For a shining time, he'd had her love and knew he'd hold it again. All the same, it was there and a sense of peace came over him.

"Look at me." She raised her face. "What do you see?"

"Love."

"Yes, anything more?"

"I don't need more."

"I'm thirty-five. My ex is forty."

"Why would you think age mattered?"

"Because my world died after Shockett won custody. He cheated with a younger homebody. I hadn't until you."

"You believe I'd think less of you because of a lost custody battle? Judge you like Ferringer? Love is all we need to see in each other."

"I slaved to get my ex through med school."

"Let the investment go. Or do you still care for him?"

"With him, time is an ally."

"Can't you start again with me."

"Middles and endings are all that remain for me."

Chapter Nine

Back at the room, Beth packed the one suitcase and overnight toiletry bag brought with enough to last the few more days planned for this—God, Herb hadn't words to name it—retreat, rendevous, soiree, sensitivity session, party, affair, encounter, disengagement, unraveling. Hatchet job felt more in keeping with the upheaval in his soul. What remained for a puppy dog to do: yap, wag its tail, whine, yelp, lick, crouch in the corner, hump a leg? Would protestation or indignation change anything? For one moment of former bliss, he'd renounce religion, abandon fatherhood, give up marriage, belly to the throne of her love. Why can't tonight transubstantiate to yesterday and the day before and the days before that?

Their embrace in the lobby was cordial. A kiss in the room hurt prior to the lobby becoming her port of exit—the wound bleeding and terminal—yes, hurt as thoroughly as overpowering sex had drawn him to his emotional knees in Key West. But the lobby was her wish, and he honored it. She insisted on being left alone on a sofa beside the exit, beside the portal to home with a doctor who for some unfathomable reason won a second chance that Herb felt was rightfully his. He couldn't leave. She insisted. His legs wouldn't move. She turned him and moved him toward the elevator. He returned to the room and ordered a double Manhattan from room service.

Sitting in an easy chair, he propped his feet on a hassock, sipped away, and watched a "Bewitched" rerun on the boob tube. By the time he finished the cocktail, a "Peyton Place" rerun nearly concluded, but he hadn't any idea of its content because reminiscence caused a blackout of sticky-fingered time. Surely the lobby was abandoned now, and he could find a comedy club on Duval or a side street where the clientele might be congenial, the music loud, dance floor ready, and the standup comic funny. As he decided to go, the door swung open, Beth walked in and sat on the bed.

Obviously Dr. Shockett found another willing homebody and renegged on his commitment, abandoned his second chance, disappointed his ex-wife. Whatever the case, his former wife had become unstrung. She clawed wildly at her abdomen again and repeated over and over, "That son of a bitch. That son of a bitch."

Two Beths sat on the bed, and he focused on one. He sat beside her and held her tight. The front of her pink pinafore was threadbare from the clawing, and easily imagined welts lurked below the cloth. His head felt like a whirlpool, and her sobbing hurt his ears. "Sh. It's okay." He pressed her cheek against his own and felt a coolness of tears. He stopped her nail's assault on the waistline. Her arms and forehead were slick with perspiration. Then as if speaking to a murmuring television, she began, "Where did he—go? Somewhere else?" Her voice became loud. "What do you mean 'somewhere else?' Who does know, for God's sake?"

Herb lumbered out, "You don't have to talk about it."

"Damn hypnotist is crazy—the bastard said I wouldn't feel anything—I believed—this is agony!" She began clawing uncontrollably. The words pinched their way through her involuntary gasps. "Couldn't you tell the birth was breach, you idiot." Her eyes were red. She placed her hands over her face. "You're butchering me—I feel—every cut—every probe," she screamed.

He felt unsure of an appropriate response except to hinder her clawing. Recovering one's savvy seemed unattainable. He thought of playing gynecologist or hypnotist in the unfolding drama. Was her delivery room a place for them to meet? Did she wish the fantasy to be his too?

"What is the hypnotist saying?" he asked.

"You're numb all over. Listen to my voice. My voice is the only one you hear." She screamed, "I'm not numb—all over—cuts—blood—mine—you butcher."

"He was incompetent, yes, a butcher," Herb said.

"God, how I screamed." She fell face down in Herb's lap. He massaged her shoulders. How hollow, empty, barren she sounded. "Years of therapy—I hate—my own daughter—my *ex*—don't you see?"

"Yes. Yes. But the baby is innocent."

"I know that, Herb," she sobbed. "It doesn't help—I wish her—dead—for what—she's done to me."

"I can't go there. I can't. Who wishes a child dead?"

She sat up abruptly. "Get away—from me!" Wildly, she clawed him, scratched his face, his arm. Drawing blood felt like a lesser pain than the turmoil of rejection. Witnessing her anguish didn't ease the whirlpool. A heart of darkness stunned him. She lashed out at a lover, at a man who worshiped her. He felt like an icon for Shockett's abandonment, a hypnotist's miscalculation, the surgeon's bungling and it cut through him. "No, " he bellowed.

And momentarily before her next assault, Herb thought Beth's grin to be sinister, her voice diabolic, her stature triumphant. "We're even, you heartless fuck," she wailed. "Stay out—stay out of my life," and stormed from the motel room in a tattered dress wet with the tears of attrition.

Chapter Ten

When Herb returned to Miami without Beth, he learned his dog had run away. Alvin had been up all night looking for her, but Winnie was no where to be found. The leash broke when boy and dog reached Alhambra Circle, and she took off. His search would have gone on if Herb hadn't seen the boy on Dixie Highway, the route Herb used from Key West. When he got in the car, Alvin was nearly incomprehensible. Herb assured him that they'd find Winnie by blowing the horn twice. Winnie usually came at that signal. This time his call remained unheeded.

On the journey to Minnesota, he would let the dog roam parking lots and gas stations. When he beeped twice, she'd return from her escapade and leap through the window into the car. He and Alvin started a radius of the neighborhood, beeping at stop signs or mid-block. Herb waited, watched, listened but no Winnie.

Before meeting Beth, he had lost Winnie. After stopping for gas somewhere between Miami and Minnesota, he drove off without beeping. Fifty miles later, he reached down to pet her. Was he so envisioning life with Mary as to forget the animal he loved? When he returned to the station over two hours later, Winnie was gone. He traveled the back road from station to station, beeping, doubting, fearing. Two kids on bikes overheard his conversation with a third gas station attendant, and said they had seen the dog twenty minutes earlier. Herb followed them down a back road and across a mown hayfield. At a fence, far side of the field, he stopped. The boys pointed toward a suburban neighborhood. Of course, thought Herb, she would look for a familiar house. At the end of a far off block, he saw her running from house to house, scratching each door. He beeped the horn. Recognizing the call, she immediately bounded toward the car, ears flapping, legs pushing the limits of her speed, tongue hanging from a dog-smile mouth. She flew from the ground like a bird taking flight, sailed through the window, and landed beside him. She licked from his face down the arm to his palm and sat only when he hugged her. On the front seat, her tail and ass wagged, beating between glove compartment and upholstery, rapid sweeps of reunited happiness. As soon as he drove off, she lay down as if nothing had happened.

Now his car circled the peripheries of Coral Gables. Its horn beeped at regular intervals. Was it possible that the animal headed for Key West? Surely he'd have seen her on his return home. Was she roaming the campus where they walked on weekends? Did she head for Venetian Island, the other home familiar to her? He bet on Venetian Island. The sound of the horn echoed through palmettos and pines, through clumps of Florida Holly; it permeated land crab dugouts along the Bayshore, looking, searching, harsh, yet, tender and loving like a human soul encased in a motel room of loneliness and desperation. Would that his Beth returned with the simple beep of a horn. Would that his emotions were calmed by such a simple signal. Would that his lover saw resentment nonexistent in him. Were endings so strong a force that they came in threes? First his dad, then his lover, now his dog. The horn bore the only connection to master and pet, and the car would run out of gas before he gave up the search. How was Herb to know that his Winnie no longer heard? Less than a mile away, she lay on a white line beside the highway, ears awry, blood beneath her head.

On a waterside drive leading to Venetian Island, he saw what he feared. On her way to mom's, he knew. His mind raced through locations of vets Winnie'd been to. He passed the animal hoping it wasn't his dog. There was a slight breathing, and he rushed to her side. The car hardly off the highway, its passenger was as vulnerable as the dog. Herb motioned for Alvin to get out. Kneeling there, the truth became clear, "Oh, God," he said as though he were at a funeral again. "She was happy, Alvin, and lived a long life." He was chokey. "Not the best way to go, but it was quick." Then, like being beside his father's body in the hospital, he gathered Winnie into his arms.

Alvin stepped back. "Great God Almighty, don't touch her, please, Mr. Herb, please. The police will come get her." The boy had a wild look about him, and the edges of his eyes glistened in the midday light.

Blood stained Herb's forearm. She was as limp and tepid as Sol had been. He carried her to the car and placed her on the seat. He opened the door for Alvin.

"No! I ain't got my root man charm, and she going to curse me sure as I done let her die." Alvin backed away.

"It's not your fault, Alvin. Stuff happens." Plaintiveness coated his plea and resentment turned inward. He should have boarded Winnie, shouldn't have been so complacent, so lax about her care. About relinquishing responsibility. What gruesome resolve came by offending a kid whose work and devotion were flawless? The dog could have been killed on the way to Minnesota or on any highway where she roamed freely. Hadn't she gotten out when the exterminator opened the door to his apartment and made it to Venetian Island to find him? Luck brought her there. This time was a fluke, cosmic irony. If there were blame, a nemesis to be avoided, Herb accepted it fully.

The kid bit at a fingernail and held his stomach as if to purge. "I ain't riding with death. It makes a spot of white hair that marks you for a lifetime. I seen them people what suffers from a curse. Can't hear and they goes blind. No way, Mr. Herb."

Herb slammed the fender with his fist. The action didn't even clear Herb's head let alone anything but heighten Alvin's anxiety. When blood beaded on a knuckle, the fist sought shelter in the warmth of Herb's mouth. As Alvin backed into the street, Herb said, "One accident is all I can take this afternoon." He extended his hand. "Come with me, please."

"Look what I done. Look what I done."

"She's a dog, not a human. Get out of the road."

"You loved her. She was off to find you."

"Please get in."

"This ain't how I wanted things to work."

"I'll come back for you."

"I be walking back. Look what I done."

"Home's too far."

"Please let me be."

"Here's cash. Call a cab." The cash flew from Herb's hand onto the swale and off into the shore brush. Neither of them made an effort to retrieve it.

"I been caring for myself without no help. Thanks but no thanks."

"Not your fault. Crap happens."

"I can't ride with death on that seat, Mr. Herb. It be calling me next."

Herb climbed into the driver's seat and waited for the boy to get in, but Alvin pushed the door closed and walked off. He was well down the road before he stopped. A tire spun in the gravel and squealed when it hit pavement. By the gravel-kicking, twisting, and flailing seen in the rear view mirror, he saw that Alvin required being alone. From this point forward, could teacher and student stand eyeball to eyeball without glancing away? At that moment, he decided to give Alvin Beth's painting. What possible joy might a spurned lover get from viewing a nightmarish memorial to rejection. Herb's eyes burned as he patted the dead animal. "So-long, my love," he whispered.

Chapter Eleven

Friar Tuck's on a Saturday night featured a wholly recovered Ira Sullivan and his quintet. Having finished a cornet solo, the leader shifted to an alto sax riff with piano, bass, drums, and trombone accompaniment from some University of Miami Jazz elite. Herb sat at the bar since all tables and booths were crammed. Some diehards weren't lucky enough to find a place and stood, drinks in hand, by the door or around the dance floor. He waved across at Otto Kraushaar, long time friend of John Phillip Sousa, and collaborator on "The Music Man," and Dean John Bitter, the man responsible for bringing Sullivan to the university school of music. The two old musicians, mentors as well, influenced curriculum, taste in music, and Herb's knowledge in that area. Chris Curry, renowned instructor of solfege, sipped a Jack Rose bought for her when she insisted the adjunct Freshmen Composition instructor sit beside her in a vacant seat. As a striking brunette in her late twenties who dressed like a pilgrim and acted as stodgy as one, she seemed out of place in the frenzy of a jazz club. Yet tonight her austere demeanor melted into an appreciative smile as she stroked Herb's forearm and listened to the jazz doctor and his group do a wild improv of "Lullaby of Birdland." Evidently perfect pitch appreciated fine-tuned progressive dissonance. When Herb asked her to dance, she declined and provoked his ear with the story that she couldn't move to music, only teach it.

Whom he least expected to see was Alvin McKinnon because the drinking age in Florida was twenty-one. The kid seated beside another, thirtyish, pudgy man waved from a table for four with two empty chairs as if guests were expected. The stranger wore dark glasses and a denim jacket which contrasted to Alvin's sleeveless white t-shirt and black vest which displayed his muscle-cut body he seemed proud to advertise in a bar. Chris promised to hold Herb's seat as he took Alvin up on the offer to sit stage side. Few experiences matched a close encounter with jazz musicians where you watched fingers fly up and down electrified keys, cheeks puff out, embouchures twist and jounce, sweat bead up on spotlighted faces gesticulating to emotional phrasing and lightening improvisation. Where else could one hear the inhalation of lung power which produced art? Why miss foot tapping, hip swaying, arched backs, and ceiling-bound brass and woodwinds? "Birdland" brought cheers from jazz afficionados. Sullivan's solo moved the crowd like wheat in a breeze. When the band came back in, people stood and applauded. Sullivan acknowledged with the sway of his instrument, and they oscillated with him.

The band broke in time for Alvin's introduction of Uncle Rufus. Seems Rufus hadn't any surname or wasn't willing to share one as well as being unimpressed with Alvin's instructor. Uncle made a point of being a dropout yet owning a fine car, his own crib, and a flock at Mt. Zion to which he preached regular without schooling. As relatives go, this one hadn't any family resemblance—must be a father's side since Alvin favored his mom—and unlike Alvin, rather husky. Rufus made it clear that the drinks which he had paid for were the last for this night and going "a-slumming" seemed foremost on uncle's lips. "A-slumming," evoked quite an array of speculations, but Herb was too liberal, esoteric, and middle class to question about practice. Most odd, uncle seemed unable to keep his hands off Alvin, even setting the boy's cocktail closer after it had been intentionally moved aside.

"Why your lady friend ain't come to meet us, Mr. Herb?" the boy asked.

"Miss Curry's saving seats."

"Miss Beth likes jazz, don't she?"

"If she were here, I don't think it'd be with me."

Rufus, more interested scratching the crotch of Friar Tuck on his cocktail napkin, inserted,"Can we go, girl?"

"Hush up, boy." Alvin removed Rufus's palm from its tour of his torso. "I knowed," the boy went on, "you two broke up when you give me the picture."

Rufus's palm snuck its way back to a shoulder. "My part's paid so now do yours, girl."

"Show some respect Rufus. I ain't telling you twice."

"It's okay Alvin. I only came to say hello. Nice meeting you Uncle Rufus."

"The pleasure is yours, man."

Once returning to the bar, he found Chris interested in coffee at Tylers, a quiet after dinner hangout for snacking and sociable faculty and students. They left her car in the Grove and took his. But the restaurant wasn't what the solfege instructor had in mind. Herb wasn't sure coffee was on his mind either. Decorum precluded asking her to his place in Coral Gables. Well before midnight, alcohol seemed a better alternative, so he suggested Fox's Inn which presented a relaxed, dark, and intimate ambiance. She lived above Maury's Garage where, if he felt so inclined, she'd mix a couple of nightcaps. What the hell, a man often makes headway complying with a woman's choices. He u-turned on Sunset Drive and headed back to Shenandoah where Chris admittedly harbored an array of popular liquors. Oddly, her place was less than a mile from Beth's and the car nearly went there of its own volition.

Offsetting about the place above Maury's Garage was an orange and black brocaded sofa
in French Provincial style upon which they sat and sipped Jack Roses, her cocktail of choice because ingredients for a Manhattan weren't in Chris's world. Harvey's Bristol Cream, Kahlua, Cream de Mint, Sloe Gin, Galliano, Vodka, Applejack Brandy (several bottles), and Bailey's Irish Cream were. The French Provincial occasional chairs across the room, also orange and velour, parenthesized a Duncan Phyfe table between them with glass miniatures all in a musical motif along with an ugly, wood metronome. In one corner, a cello and bow sat beside a medieval midwife chair as if practice were momentarily suspended. The walls held cheap reproductions of English landscapes by Constable and Turner, symmetrical and evenly hung while above the passthrough to the kitchen a large treble clef done in silver

plastic faced some quarter notes.

"Why did you drop your music major?" Chris was asking as the stereo sang some Dave Brubeck as if jazz were the sum total of her idea of Herb's musical taste.

"Madam Zogarian's solfege class, to be exact," he admitted.

"Was my predecessor that bad?"

"Quite good, actually, for me to realize I hadn't any ear."

"What is your ear good for?"

"Listening."

Admissibly, Chris believed sensitive guys understood the importance of insightful listening for a harmonious relationship. Men, she thought, walked away from discord which required adjustments of tonality between couples so that harmony prevailed. "Life is melody," she went on, "and listening to and appreciating a female's song seems a performance so few of your gender are truly capable." And Herb listened as she went into her song of being raised in Coral Gables—to be precise, by the Currys of Coral Gables, a family emanating from Plymouth. Her father belonged to Mensa—she'd get him to sponsor Herb if interested in becoming a member—and did charity work as a Junior Miss when her mother served as Coral Gables Women's Club President. Their heritage qualified mother and daughter for membership in the DAR, and they assisted with fund raising efforts of the Merrick Society until Chris learned of George Merrick's anti-Semitic leanings. He belonged to the restricted Men's Bath Club on Miami Beach and insisted that the city he founded refuse to sell property to Coloreds and Jews. Her father headed pediatrics at Doctor's Hospital, a true healer in the Curry tradition. Chris's doctorate in music ended a longstanding line of physicians, but she literally fainted at the sight of blood. And on she went until Herb leaned in and kissed her more to stop the onslaught of personal genealogy than from desire.

If remembrance served correctly, he carried Beth into her bedroom on an initial date. She felt warm and supple in his arms, and like their dance-floor grace at Friar Tuck's, they glided into lovemaking as if tresses, flesh, lips, hands, limbs, and bodies played a symphony of the heart and mind. When they melded together beginnings and endings faded, time and motion became seamless. In this scenario, Chris impounded his hand and pulled him through the doorway to her bedroom, removed his clothes, undressed herself, and lay like a sacrificial lamb at the altar with the high priest standing above her. When he knelt into an embrace, she jerked up and a collision of foreheads started a litany of apologies. He asked if she might scoot over so that he could lie beside her which when done began some petting and decisive maneuvering whereby she squirmed spreadeagle under him like it or not. With both hands tugging at his buttocks and lips pecking at his mouth like a chicken eating corn, he tried, God, he tried to listen to her music, find her harmony, play her melody, sound some chords, but his manhood refused to cooperate.

Chris was not by any means a bad looking girl. Quite the contrary, her locks were soft and flowing, features *a la* Rita Moreno, olive skin enticing and smooth, breasts petite, firm, warm to the touch, hips nicely rounded, stomach flat, perfume lightly floral, in short, everything a man might desire, yet Peter didn't think so. If humiliation came as a voyeur to gawk, Herb would, of necessity, introduce him. Did he dare, amid all this activity, reach down to help the guy out? Kisses raised her stakes as moaning and panting accompanied the slapping of bodies while he felt crippled by a sympathetic nympho whose palms pulled at his buttocks. The fuel-less engine slowed, faltered, and stopped. Rolling off the rack, he apologized. She, like a genteel lady of breeding, offered that it didn't matter, not to worry. Liquor—especially Jack Roses—do that to a man.

"I don't know what's wrong." He sat on the edge of the bed and awaited a caustic remark, but all she said was, "Liquor is a depressant. Don't worry. It's okay. I understand."

"I don't."

"Alcohol does that to men." And so on until disaster became embarrassment like a patient growing stable and emotionally functional. Chris covered herself with a sheet while Herb dressed. The stereo now played some Kenton—*Laura*—a rendition which would fall from his list of favorites. "You can let yourself out," she said. "Thanks for coming."

Chapter Twelve

If this were drunkenness, why did the car travel unswervingly and at normal speed, why was his head clear, thinking un-muddled, emotions repressed, his reflexes normal? Jack Rose aside, he'd had very few drinks at Friar Tucks. So why was the car headed to Beth's place? What stopped him from gong home? Why did the headlights go out a block before the car concealed itself under a spreading Ficus in a yard across from her house. A strange gray Cadillac sat beside her Datsun in the driveway taking a space once reserved for him. Shades on the livingroom bay windows showed silhouettes sporadically moving. He watched from the driver's seat and wished he had binoculars. Beth's silhouette he recognized by the long, straight hair, graceful saunter, and slender figure. She twisted her hair into a bun and fixed it atop her head—something matronly he'd never seen her do. A second girl, a shorter version, carried slippers in her hand which were too big to be hers. The man, a doctor, a healer seemed generic—slightly over six feet tall, a halo of hair around a bald scalp, formal clothes—wearing a jacket or blazer—long legs, short torso, concave chest, and a moustache. He handed a small box taken from an inside pocket to someone off the silhouette screen. Twice the doctor bent toward the shade as if putting out a cigarette in an ashtray. The surveillance man outside once knew there were no ashtrays from his memory of the inside looking out. As if drawn by disgust or jealousy, Herb found himself ass to fender as if a drug bust were minutes away and the stakeout progressing toward an arrest. What could he do if just one embrace silhouetted itself on the shades? If he crawled between low hedges and the windows, he could spy under the blinds which a desperate mind believed necessary. If he knocked on the door in the middle of the night, what would that accomplish except a call to the police? Damn car had no business bringing him here to begin with. This act was one of obsession, lack of discipline, or self-pitying excess. Biting hard on his lower lip might shock his senses to reality. His lover had cut him off. Hiding behind the hedges loomed as a next insanity had not a police cruiser snuck into the scene unannounced.

Because the darkened house behind the Ficus contained a nervous occupant who slept lightly, two Metro-Dade Officers flanked him and asked for identification and explanation. Herb's truthful account got him handcuffed and led to Beth's porch. Dr. Shockett stepped out closing the door behind him, said, *yes*, he knew the stalker, and, *yes,* cart him off to jail because charges would certainly be filed. Handcuffed and sitting in the back seat of a police cage smacked of trouble which Beth never came out to resolve. With the police report completed, Herb got taxi service to Dade County Jail. Having one's freedom usurped, getting fingerprinted, having a breathalyser test, and being locked up were ends that certainly did not justify the indiscretion of his tangential behavior. For Pete's sake, hadn't he suffered enough humiliation tonight? Charges of stalking and loitering had more of a stigma than driving under the influence, but Herb wasn't driving when arrested. His car got impounded, his ass thrown into a cell within a cell where prisoners had full view of him like a monkey at a zoo.

The whole night, arms reached through the bars trying to get at him. Reached from all sides. And the gawkers had plenty to tell about the Dade County Jail. This was the self-same cell where old Darby McPhee croaked after a fist-infested interrogation several nights before; the cell where Randy Foster went off the deep end then to the funny farm; the self-same place where Jackson Reed bled to death from an inmate's knife-wound to the neck; the hole where cursed others got syphilis, genital herpes, and prick rot from holding the bars or sitting on the floor. And arms with powerful hands reached for Herb from all directions—muscled arms, some hairy, others slick; black and white ones, some slender or with scars or freckles; Latino and Seminole ones, decked with watches, id bracelets, tattoos—an anchor with a heart, fire-breathing dragon, lightning. The guys wanted to feel the expensive cloth of his clothes. Could they try on his designer shoes? Touch his beauty-shop hair. Could he spare a cigarette? Arms reaching through from all sides kept the novice prisoner on the floor in the center of his cell. Herb was scared shitless but too embarrassed to call for help, especially the family lawyer, and, if the authorities kept him beyond the weekend, he'd explain away his absence at the university somehow. How long could they keep him incarcerated? This was America, for God's sake.

In court the next day, Judge Snowden set bail which Herb paid through an attending bondsman in a heartbeat to gain his own release. The judge stated that courts didn't look kindly on perverts who stalked women and children. The plaintiff had been mortified by the abominable behavior. And if guilty, the judge apprised Herb of the maximum fine and imprisonment allowed by law. An ambulance chaser at Snowden's proceedings took the opportunity for a handsome retainer to prepare a reasonable defense. And Herb was in a cab headed for the impound lot to retrieve his Continental. However, before reaching trial, the charges were dropped. The embarrassment and lesson lingered. So did the fear fellow prisoners evoked during that one night in solitary. Herb dreamed for a month about arms reaching for his clothes, shoes, and throat.

Chapter Thirteen

Once again Herb found himself before the throne of Lola May Ferringer, bare walls, blowup of Boman F. Ashe, and all. She knew of his arrest, the booking, and probably the dropped charges not because the university checked police and court records but because someone informed her of the incident. Herb chose to believe the good Doctor Shockett wanted him off campus and away from Beth when, in fact, the American Lit Professor did her own telling to Lola May. But spurned lovers disbelieve such cruel actions even with proof. They are incapable of accepting endings, living apart, losing to fate. They exist in a universe of hope and despair. In this case, negatives would not have altered Herb's obsessive love. And the weekend incident at Beth's home was none of Ferringer's business.

The VP's hands were clasped tightly and her lips pursed below the glare of hazel eyes behind bifocals. "I think you need not report to teaching duties for your next class or any thereafter," she said.

Herb leaned onto the sacred space of his desk. "Is there no due process here?"

"This is a private institution supported by donors who demand vigilance."

"Miss Ferringer, the charges were dropped."

"The decision is final, Mr. Rizer."

"On what grounds am I being dismissed?"

"Moral impropriety."

"That would, indeed, indict you as well for an indiscreet weekend in the Keys with Barry Whorton. Not so?"

"My personal life is none of your affair."

"Mine is not yours, Miss Ferringer."

She motioned for him to remove his elbows from her desk. "I felt from the outset you were poison in the lifeblood of this university."

Leaning back, he folded his arms across his chest.

"Isn't that somewhat unobjective?"

"Going to jail for loitering isn't. Can't we end this unpleasantness? Please go." She shooed him like a cook chasing flies. When he didn't move, she added, "Shall I call security?"

"You'll force me to share biases with the Anti Defamation League."

"Close the door on your way out, sir."

"The notoriety might be detrimental in a community with prominent Jewish philanthropists. If you shun us, Miss Ferringer, then reject our money." Herb had the vice president transfixed. "I could give you a list of prominent donors from the congregation at Temple Emanu-El. Then there's the Miami Business League which contributes handsomely to university coffers. Among them are Jewish owners of major department stores, drug chains, discount houses, jewelry exchanges, and other successful businesses. My dad and others in the Hotel Owners' Association endowed this university with scholarship funds. Didn't Baron de Hirshmeyer donate your law school?"

"Well, sir, you've done impressive research. Then again, I'm versed in your outlandish assignments. Do you intend to blackmail the university for personal gain, sir?"

"Only its vice president of ill will."

"No one at this institution is inclined toward your continued employment. And I resent your innuendo."

"I resent your unwarranted persecution. Am I to understand that my next class and each one thereafter has the same adjunct professor it started with?"

"For your ilk, we offer buying out a contract as more to your liking—and ours as well."

"I don't have a contract."

"Are you so naive as to not perceive my meaning?"

"Money isn't a concern. In lieu of paying me off, I'll resume my present position, thank you. So get the hell off my back."

"I am unaccustomed to foul language in my presence. Especially from an English instructor if I am not stretching

64

the meaning here. Please, for a lady of breeding, mind the manners which should have been part of your upbringing."

"What's your decision, Miss Ferringer? My day or your way?"

"For the moment, sir, you prevail. This dismissal is on hold. You are excused. Do me the courtesy of closing the door on your way out."

"The damn thing needs a hydraulic apparatus so you don't need to repeat yourself." Herb left the door open.

Thinking the arrest to be settled both professionally and legally, Herb was surprised by a temporary restraining order from Judge Snowden's court. The sheriff delivered the document to his apartment around five shortly before the cancelled proceedings of his stalking and loitering hearing. The order forbade him to be near or about Mrs. Shockett's domestic premises, make any contact by phone or in person, or arrange any third party contact. The list of harassments suffered by the plaintiff within the document were bogus except for the night under the Ficus which got him arrested. It was outrageous that he supposedly threatened Samantha, Beth's daughter, when he never met the girl in his life. But anger served no purpose, and he decided to accept the legal service from the Sheriff without question and waive any hearing rights to counter the claims. Whatever was right seemed wrong, day was night and visa-versa, love became a scratch on the face, a rebuff (*we're even, fuck*), a rejection (*stay out of my life*), a restraining order, a distant stare, a downcast eye, false accusations, and hurt transposing into heartbreak, self-reproach, and self-pity.

What saved Herb from himself was the classroom. The mid term exam which the department prepared with no input from a lovelorn adjunct came and went with Herb's freshmen scoring higher than any other sections of Freshman Composition. His progressive methods worked. A football player of his now wrote profiles for the campus paper, the *Miami Herald* published submissions from his financial aide group in their "Tropic Magazine," Alvin won a Rotary Club essay contest—America: Land of Freedom, and the literary magazine, *Ibis*, chose a scholarship athlete and other freshman fiction from his proteges. His office hours were booked with emerging scholars. Pupils lunched with him at the Student Union where they read, discussed, and analyzed prose styles of Virginia Woolf, Henry David Thoreau, and E. B. White. A particular passage from White's essay, "Here's New York City," Herb brought to a discussion. "The city, for the first time in its long history, is destructible. A single flight of planes no bigger than a wedge of geese can quickly end this island fantasy, burn the towers, crumble the bridges, turn the underground passages into lethal chambers, cremate the millions. The intimation of mortality is part of New York in the sound of the jets overhead, in the black headlines of the latest edition." He challenged students to use a prophetic eye from their view of now. He assigned "By the Waters of Babylon," which became a hot topic. Alvin wrote a fine paper on the cold war citing White and Bene't and excerpts appeared in *Miami Times* and then picked up by the *Miami Daily News* whose editor, Bill Baggs, sent the boy a congratulations note with a check.

Herb also began a critique group at the Coral Gables Library. The outreach program brought seniors and youth together. Not unexpectedly, a coterie from student government placed his name in contention for professor of the year, the first time in university history an adjunct was nominated for the honor. The time seemed right to approach Max Alvarez for a full time position. And under the positive circumstances, the Dean of Arts and Sciences granted his request for second semester by combining slated adjunct and graduate assigned courses into one full time schedule. Silence from Lola May Ferringer did not daunt her mission.

However, day's end had emptiness, remorse, and frustrations which grew exponentially. Whatever lyricists wrote *love's a hurting thing, cheating heart, letter of goodbye, broken hearted, only you, or crying shame* called to Herb when not immersed in work to join their ranks. *Bleeding heart, crying after midnight, lonely boy* were lyrics he added to their books. Alvin sensed his prof's pain and suggested a diversion, mid day basketball, one on one, and workouts at the university gym when Alvin's job schedule permitted. Within a month, Herb dropped body mass and looked like a lightweight boxer.

One afternoon as they assisted each other with weight lifting, a fight broke out in the gym. Two linebackers, dorm mates, argued about a coed. Not clear what the run-in was, it elevated at the shout of *she's a whore*. The football players shoved. A loud slam against the lockers reverberated and turned heads. Then one flashed a switch blade that sprung open to broadcast its outrage. When coach saw it, he ran for help. A throng encircled as the one linebacker wrapped a towel around his forearm. He egged his assailant on. Curses flew, voices shouted, eyes flared, arms swung, and bodies circled like cocks in a ring. The towel blocked the blade and a free fist caught the wild eyed stabber in the jaw. The crowd whooped. They ooh-ed when a second punch hit home. On a rebound, the stabber did a three-sixty, and the knife plunged home into an upper arm. Its bloody blade flashed in the florescent light. It swooped for a second blow to the chest. The towel blocked it. Blood oozed as the wounded guy drew back. That's when Herb grabbed the would be killer, lifted him from behind, griped his wrist, and slammed it against the lockers. The knife sailed across the room and spun over a steel drain. It rattled like pebbles on a tin roof. The wounded boy went for it, but Alvin grabbed the knife and took off. "Calm down, calm down, fellow," Herb said again and again. He body hugged the linebacker until the boy complied. From there, the coach took over. Later, he told Herb that it was nuts to get between guys with knives, but thanked him for intervening before someone got seriously hurt or killed. Alvin said, "You was scared as me, Mr. Herb. Why'd you take a chance like that?" Herb hadn't any explanation for his action, so all he said was, "because no one else did."

Student and professor took a hiatus from the gym after that and began bar hopping and "a-slummin'," as Alvin called it. The young man introduced Herb to a hotspot, the

Sir John Club, where rhythm and blues reigned supreme. Herb got blown away with some of the head liners at the club like Ruth Brown, Rufus Thomas, Big Mama Thornton, Jimmy Reed, and one white woman who won favor with some rhythm and blues fans, Janis Joplin.

Herb shared his first impression of Joplin's single recording of *Ball and Chain*, and Chris Curry asked if he just got off the banana boat. Joplin, she informed him, was the greatest blues singer since Bessie Smith and implored Herb for a chance to hear the liberated star in person. "Are you sure she's appearing at the Sir John Club, in Miami, you believe next weekend, and, oh, by the way, why hasn't the *Herald* or the *News* covered her engagement? Not one word in 'About Town.'" To which Herb offered, "*Miami Times* ran a full page spread, gorgeous. But I guess Joplin's 'a-slummin',' as Alvin calls it, so the mainstream press overlooked her." Chris never read *Miami Times* or heard of the Sir John. Was she aware of its clientele's contrast to the citizenry of Coral Gables and its Women's Club, its DAR? Could she take its Overtown location? Did she care that Herb, she and Janis might be the only white faces in the juke joint? Take me there and find out was her reply.

So Friday after classes, Herb met Chris, Alvin, and Uncle Rufus at Tyler's Restaurant. Since Alvin advised Herb not to go "a-slummin'" without no bro in tow, the white folks followed the dark folks down US One and across the Miami River Bridge to Overtown and the Sir John Club which lay close to the river. All but a few streetlights around the club were broken, and a junk Chevy without wheels and shattered glass sat by the curb. Herb parked his Continental in a chain-linked lot beside Alvin's antique Ford truck. The crushed rock and patches of crab grass gave the impression of wasteland. There were beer cans and broken bottles strewn about. Once on the sidewalk, they stepped around missing chunks of concrete and a crack which a now dead tree root raised as nature's protest. The tree itself had been struck by lightning and split down the middle.

The foursome crossed the street toward a one story,

black building with CBS blocked in windows and a blue neon top hat and red cane with a bright, white Sir John scrawled across them. A fancy, hand painted poster with an eight-by-ten glossy of Janis Joplin announced the featured entertainer. The solid metal door had an electronic lock which buzzed open. A bruiser, tall enough to be a Harlem Globe Trotter but too hefty for one, guarded the inner cage and collected cover charges, a dollar a head. He stood behind an elbow-high, barred window and buzzed the group into a dark hallway but not without a wink and a "Hey, mama," to Chris. As Alvin passed, the bouncer rumbled in bass tones, "She be right fine."

The Sir John had a large, u-shaped bar surrounding a raised stage atop its mirrored shelves. The only familiar liquor Herb saw on the sparse shelves was Southern Comfort, Four Feathers, Clan McGreggor, Outrigger. Others were brands he didn't know existed. He walked under a batten of Fresnels and spots which illuminated a guitarist with graying beard and a red bandana who tapped and strummed a story of *store bought, home brought, crated and dated, ba-lues.* Tables and chairs beyond the bar as well as the concrete floor and walls were all black with a standard mirror-ball refracting rainbow colors throughout a room which seated over a hundred within a cramped arrangement. Above, circular appendages also done in black crisscrossed the room to throw some cool air on the sweaty crowd. Among white eyeballs and glistening choppers, Herb determined the patrons to be mostly young and all black. Except for an occasional redhead or bleach job, hair fused into the hell-like decor. The warehouse-height ceiling had burlap draped from one end to the other, and narrow-beam spots hit myriad surfaces without any pattern much like sporadic, heavy raindrops dot a sidewalk before a storm. As Alvin paraded through the shafts of light for a place to sit, his pale-faced anomalies, namely, Herb and Chris, got some eyeing. One girl said under breath, "You be a-slummin', girl?" as Chris passed. When Herb glanced back, faces fell or turned, girls shifted in their seats, guys leaned back and looked up.

One crowded area had the pungent scent of marijuana. Another smelled of stale bourbon, one of Gardenia perfume, then hay, then Jasmine. A time or two Herb inhaled a unique scent that bigots on both sides of the color divide claimed as rank. Honkies smell sour blacks claimed. Coloreds smell like rotten eggs whites claimed. Interracial advocates denied any body odors while reasonable people with olfactory senses in tact understood and smelled it. Perhaps it was a scent endemic to arousal, or sweat stored from intense activity, or oils from hygienically lazy people. Along with the body odor was the unmistakable haze of cigarette smoke which the cooling system appeared incapable of removing.

The table Alvin found had only three raffia-woven chairs so Herb and Chris shared one back to back until some lanky dude with a black leather cabby hat, satin, royal blue shirt, and ostentatious gold-plated neck-chain with a Jesus-on-the-cross dangling above his bare sternum offered his chair and went off to find another.

When a waitress came and Chris ordered her usual Jack Rose, an instant of shocked, offended routine caused the girl to pause before breaking into a broad, white-toothed smile. She jutted out her short-skirted hip, rested a fisted and crooked arm on it, puckered up and said, "You thinking this be some Saturday social, mama," to which Chris came back with, "A bourbon on the rocks will do," and got a, "Now you're a talking, girl." Herb gave the waitress a ten for all four drinks and said to keep the change which kept her close to the table for refills.

Uncle Rufus came with a first guffaw. "A Jack Rose, please?" He had an impressive mimic of white dialect. "Sakes alive, you white folks taking us through some changes."

Alvin punched Rufus's arm then bumped heads gently. "Mr. Herb, my uncle ain't seen nor heard tell of Applejack Brandy. Whiskey be closest to mixed company he come."

Rufus fired back in a hellfire tone, "How you know what I know. Now, you going through some changes, girl.

And don't hit me no more."

"Ain't changes like you sees it, nigger," Alvin said. "Black and white hears the same music with some different ears, is all."

Rufus snapped his fingers in rhythm to the blues soloist on stage. "Black ones got jive. The Man's don't." He pouted down his bottom lip then patted Alvin's head. "Some hair processing and skin bleaching say you think black ain't beautiful, girl."

"Talking like you is, sure be hateful."

"You done forgot your place, girl, bringing uppity ofays down home to black and blues shit."

Chris glared at Rufus and Herb added, "Sharing cultures breaks a cycle of ignorance on both sides of the racial divide, Rufus."

"Man, we simple folk don't know college words like *racial divide*," Uncle Rufus mimicked with Herb's middle class intonation.

"Give me your hand, Rufus," Herb said. Reluctantly, Rufus took the handshake now held between both of Herb's palms. "Warm, red blood runs through both of us. Ease up. Friends, guy?" A slight pull away caused Herb to clasp tighter. Rufus wasn't any match for Herb's gym developed grip. "For Alvin's sake." And that brought Alvin's and Chris's palms into a pile at the center of the table. The waitress and drinks stood by like a wife walking in on an extramarital affair. "You all come to hold hands or party?" she asked and waited for a pullback which uncluttered her professional serving space. She sashayed over to Herb with a Southern Comfort on the rocks and smiled, "Anything you want, honey child, just ask Lakisha."

"Bring me a double," he said.

The waitress came back before the blues singer finished his next song and took Herb's empty.

"When's Janis Joplin on?" Chris asked.

"Drink up, mama, and she'll come sooner than later."

"Whose that guy on stage?"

"Back Alley, why, he be jumping and jiving at the Sir

John since Genesis."

"I never came across the name Back Alley or his songs," Chris said.

"Don't disrespect him cause you never heard his singing. Just listen awhile."

"No one else seems to."

"He own the place, woman. He that bad?"

"Oh, please. No offense. Actually, I like his Macon style."

Again Rufus started snapping fingers. "Got some soul but them lame lyrics and a voice that done croaked like a dying frog," he said.

The waitress jutted her hip. "Ragging'll get a free drink or two for sure, boy," Lakisha said.

"Never you mind a telling him what I say. How come I ain't seen you in church, Mt. Zion, over that-a-way." Rufus pointed toward the north wall.

Lakisha laughed. "Me and preaching parted company back of a barn in Eatonville."

"Lakisha Brown?"

"Sure as I'm standing here."

"But for the dark in here, I should of knowed a down home gal. Your little girl grown now?"

"How you know my Sassy?"

Rufus smiled for the first time. "Clarence Jackson my cousin."

"You be Firefly Rufus." She laughed. "Orlando police still hunting for a Muslim burned their Jewish church. Any home boys know you in Miami?"

Back came the frown. "Yeah. Well. That story be Jew-lady jawing."

Lakisha wiped the table and took Herb's empty. "Another double, Mister?"

He nodded.

"Lord, Firefly, now you firing up folks right here under our black noses?"

"Come by my church. I done quit The Nation of Islam. Been born again and witnessing."

72

"Another round, Lakisha, for everybody including Jew-lady Rufus," Herb said doling out another tenner. And off she went.

Rufus's lip went down again big time, and he folded his arms across his chest. "What you mean, honky, by Jew-lady Rufus?"

Herb spoke somewhat louder than expected. "Look around, my boy. See anyone who's offended?"

Rufus leaned back. "Me. For one."

"Why, my boy, being Jewish is a good thing. For one, you make money, right?"

Now Rufus turned to Alvin likely for support because brothers stuck together. "Call Sammy Davis a Jew boy, not me," he sneered.

"I've been called a Jew," Herb said as he flashed a gold Mogen David from under his shirt.

Rufus hadn't any idea of the symbol. "Won't put no disrespect on Alvin's teacher-man."

"But I'm all horns and cheep—sitting right here before your biased eyes."

"Oh, man. You a Jew?"

"What's wrong, Firefly? You looked pissed."

At this point, Rufus put his arms around Alvin and Herb and raised his eyes toward the heavens which in this place was a cloud of cigarette smoke and black burlap sprinkled with man made stars. He began with, "Jesus, forgive Mr. Herb his sins. Take him into your bosom, Lord, and save him from eternal fire. Join hands and pray for deliverance. God Almighty, pluck out the evil in your servant's mind." His platitudes carried to the adjacent table of patrons.

"Hey, preacher, let Sunday come-to-prayer folks have you some fun tonight. Keep Jesus where he belong, in church or hanging round your neck. This be the Sir John, not Saint John," said the cabby hatted, cross-wearing dude in his newfound chair.

Chris clapped and Alvin cupped a hand around her ear and said something that made her laugh. Herb leaned toward

Rufus and sneered into his ear, "First off, it pisses me off that you're so cock sure all answers lie only in your religion. Second, convert your hate to love if you think to convert. You define bad taste. And, shithead, you need to reconsider who the sinner is in your prayer." With that, Rufus grabbed Alvin and towed him toward the men's room yakking angrily on the way.

Then all hell broke loose as Janis Joplin sauntered onto the stage. Applause, hoops, hollers, and calls started at the bar and spread. A drummer, players of piano, keyboard, and guitar took the stage behind her. Back Alley helped Joplin adjust the mike, and got a big hug from the star as he humbled off. Chris was first out of her seat calling, "Sing 'Ball and Chain,' Janis. Sing 'Ball and Chain.'" Janis Joplin pointed a finger halfway across the tumultuous room, jangled a stack of baubles round a wrist, clacked them against the mike, and gave a wink from behind those huge, round glasses hugging her chubby cheeks and big-mouthed smile. Was "Ball and Chain" the planned opener or was Chris its catalyst? The crowd chanted, "Ball and Chain, Ball and Chain," to a sort of rhythmic, musical teaser which uninhibited the singer. Then the Full Tilt Boogie Band broke loose at an energetic, rhythmic, seat dancing, clapping crowd and the room became electrified as a fierce, raunchy, full bodied voice wailed out Big Mama Thornton's old hit. Chris looked as if climbing on her chair might get her closer to the band's Haight-Ashbury sound. As it was, she sat on her hams. Joplin in high black boots stomped and strutted, lavender corduroy hip-huggers gyrated along with a silky, white belly, and unfettered breasts which peeked out from a black and gold spangly blouse fastened immodestly. Her persona animated the room like no other Herb had ever witnessed at the Met, La Scala, at Carnegie, Lincoln Center, or on Broadway. The raw talent and gravelly quality went straight for one's emotional home and barged through like addicts after smack. Janis Joplin came from inside her song, and stayed there for the next song and the next, never coming out, never letting emotional clutches relax until a final release. For twenty or so minutes the crowd swayed, jostled, and pumped, stood with their applause, sat appreciatively at the next intro, sang along with parts they recognized, clapped hands, cat-called, and devoured the rock and blues like lions at a kill. And Chris was on the leading edge of responses as though she and Janis Joplin were the only people in the room. The music prof had unraveled off a scarf and waved it through the air like a flag of surrender.

Janis sauntered off stage as unassumingly as entering, and the crowd rose to its feet, cheering, applauding, stomping, calling, screaming, begging for an encore until the stage lights dimmed and a DJ began some "Funky Chicken." Herb lost his Southern Comfort to a petite hand that forced it from his lips to the table and dragged him off. Being on the dance floor with Chris had to be an awkward event, but he felt loose, woozy enough not to care when she wiggled into the midst of movers, shakers, grinders, and pumpers. She jerked like a fish on pavement but managed not to step on her own toes or his. When Mr. Jesus-on-the-cross in his royal blue satin took over her dancing lessons, Herb wobbled his way back to a quickly downed Southern Comfort and watched Alvin dance his way around Uncle Rufus like Sammy Davis Junior around Quasimodo. Luckily he sat to ogle the pumping vaginas, shimmying breasts, expressive arms, bouncing Afros, stiff processes becoming loose, and wavy locks un-waving or he might have fallen. It was difficult enough to stay in a chair. Herb's Sir John Club began to turn and sway like the mirrored ball in its center.

When Lakisha brought another bourbon, she went, "Think you be having a last one, honey child?" He handed her his wallet from which she took needed bills, and stuffed it into his shirt pocket. As she disappeared into a maze of customers, Herb slid under the table and held on to its center post like a child on a carousel. Somehow his cocktail found its way onto a chair and reaching for it, he sloshed the damn thing and wet his bellbottoms. The stomp, stomp, stomp from a wooden dance floor quickened his heart and thundered in his head. His vision blurred as he guzzled some booze. In his mind's eye, a slender blond lay beneath him and the heat of their bodies meshed. They were in a bed with fertility goddesses surrounding them. What he lost in that moment in time, that first night in Beth's bed wasn't only his virginity. That miraculous evening, she gave him affirmation, spirit, confidence, and love. The sense of it still waited in his palms, lips, and body. What didn't he give in return that sent her back to the concave chest, spindly legs, and skinny body of a middle-aged doctor who dumped her once and would again?

For her love, Herb'd have become a soul mate, leaping, lurching, rising, falling on a carved horse, unfrightened of the calliope and its deafening um-pa-pa whistles. For love, he'd have paid admission, helped Beth ride, strapped her in, and stood beside her forever. For love, he'd have wandered a wild fairground to find a peaceful home, not apart but together. As he breathed, he held the life post grounding a round tabletop to the floor. As he inhaled the stale odor of a dirty floor, as he heard rhythms of the dance, he felt he and his only love breathing together, breathing as one for an unforgettable moment frozen in his memory. She spoke to him, asked after his needs, wanted to sooth his descent into melancholy, stop his surreal woe; her arms embraced him and loosened his grip on the carousel so as to be closer, to feel his loving warmth, to lean into the lifting of sorrow . What became unclear, muddled, illusory was how Beth Shockett transformed into Alvin McKinnon on a concrete floor beneath a table the night Herb senselessly closed a chapter at the Sir John Club.

Chapter Fourteen

Herb held on to snippets of sidewalk, threats hurled at Uncle Rufus, got off an uppercut to the chubby jaw that sent the Black Muslim somewhere other than here and now, saw bloody knuckles wiped onto his new paisley shirt, recalled folding into a Buddha position across from the Sir John Club, waited for the carousel ride to stop at his heady amusement park, and then keeled over. He held on to pieces of reality while stumbling along, no, being dragged along parking lot gravel by Alvin and Chris. Why didn't they leave a drunk in the dirt? The humiliation overwhelmed him. Chris agreed to drive his car home as Alvin folded him onto the front seat of the Ford. Then came some repartee between drivers as to the missing hubcaps on the Continental, its flashing lights, and intermittent horn which Alvin quieted with Herb's remote before handing the keys over to Chris. Also, the car had only one un-smashed eye lighting its exit from Overtown.

The truck wanted to stay for Sir John's late, late show, but Alvin kept cranking until the old motor revved up. When the boy turned his head around to back out, Herb pulled the comb from Alvin's cropped Afro to use for a back-scratch. Alvin's "Hey, man," came back fast, "don't mess with a brother's pick," and as quickly as the grooming device got snatched, that's how fast it went back. By now the old Ford heated its way down sixth avenue, and fumes weaseled in from under the dash or through holes in the floorboard. Herb opened the door, put one foot on the running board, leaned out and hurled sour liquid on the moving tarmac. "Thinks, Elvin. I'm getting out," he said and brought his other leg around. The truck swerved vehemently, Herb's shirt did a tight, choke hold, his butt slid to the center of the seat, and his ankles would have been severely bruised were they outside when the door slammed during what felt like a near rollover. "Stay put, Mr. Herb. We going to get you some high test coffee."

"I'm frine, Alvin," he said. "Just nude some fish air."

His stomach felt like Dresden during the bombing. And the foul fumes kept blasting in.

"Stay put, Mr. Herb."

"Fish air, fish air," he said feeling the rumble of another onslaught of nausea, and pulling away, thrust his head out the window a moment before the rear fender got a slime-shine. In every young lifetime, firsts come like a surprise party. At this one, Herb brought intoxication, inhibition, chagrin, and fuzzy inner turmoil. He knew about happenings around him, but seemed unable to cause or effect them, if, in fact, any serviceable coordination remained between brain and muscles. His eyes stung from headlights of oncoming traffic, from streetlights, stop-lights, neon signs, even stores that still had lights on inside; his ears hurt from the truck's squeaky brakes, its rusty muffler-wounded engine, car horns that yelled for attention, even buzzes from electric boxes that changed the stop-lights, powered streetlights, ran neons.

Alvin came to the surprise party with tolerance, servility, egalitarianism, overworked biceps, and a mishandled hair pick. Why would a Jew put a black guy though such a trial? Was he testing humanity? His own endurance? Destroying social boundaries? Or merely practicing self-punishment spurned lovers are prone to? If one is unable to care for himself, why not leave him in the street like so many sots who sleep in doorways or on a sidewalk in places like the Bowery or Bayfront Park or myriad skid rows inner cities are known for? Does money measure a man's worth? Help those who have, abandon those who haven't. In this compromising condition, one thing became clear to our teacher hero. Being another person's ward felt damn good. Shirking personal responsibility felt damn good. And most important, being catered to by a buddy instead of catering to anyone, catering to Beth–a specific anyone—felt damn, damn good.

Although able to walk with reasonable stability since purging, he accepted Alvin's help into the Mediterranean lobby and up posh, carpeted stairs into a familiar, lonely livingroom of a once dog-happy apartment. Deposited into a dining room armchair, he felt heartsick and pathetic while Alvin percolated coffee as if the boy had come home with a drunk brother. He didn't search for beans, the grinder, or cups like a stranger, but moved adeptly in the kitchen like a long time resident. Was it possible these two men crossed cultural, racial, religious divides because of one oil painting on canvass, a gift, a tossing away of unwanted memories? Preternaturally enduring, this payback for validation came because of a shared overflow of emotion, one artist inspiring another. What did the mentor now owe for services?

The coffee tasted rich and strong—a Jamaican Blue Mountain Blend—and Alvin steadied the mug as the warm liquid stirred senses that had temporarily gone on vacation. That humane chocolate hand gently tilted the vanilla cup onto Herb's lips while the other steadied his head. Would the caffeine help raise leaden eyelids? Could the attentive caretaker now trust the invalid prof to his own recognizance? After another cup equally administered, Herb felt a favorite down pillow under his head in a foam rubber bed his father bought when a care giving son came home to Miami. Herb's shoes clunked on the floor, adept hands unbuckled his belt, whiskey smelling pants drifted away, and his unbuttoned shirt slid up his back, over his head, and down his arms. A Peter Maxx sheet spread under his chin and a familiar tenor voice said, "Don't worry none, Mr. Herb, cause Alvin be taking special care. You my main man now."

Whether saying or thinking a *thanks*, he wasn't sure. Nausea went north for the summer, and sleep came easily. How long unconsciousness lasted was mysterious as he drifted toward awareness with an overwhelming feeling that he wasn't alone. The bedroom was completely dark. His nightlight must have burned out. The shades and curtains blacked out the Coral Gables street lights. No light came under the door either. There was something warm on his stomach. Could he have wet himself? Then he heard breathing other than his own. A palm lay on his abdomen, and it wasn't his own. He felt a twitch of fingers. A warm body radiated beside him and a leg lay across his. Would his eyes have been able to see, surely they'd witness someone. But who? It was so dark, yet he remembered Alvin undressing him. His head throbbed painfully. Was it terrible if the boy decided that driving himself home in the early hours was as impractical as sleeping on the floor or on the divan instead of this king-sized bed? Pulsing—thwack, thwack—his brain wished to explode. In a drunken state, had he acted inappropriately so that the boy felt comfortable sprawled across his pal? *What immodesty happened during his alcoholic stupor,* he wondered. The pounding, achy brain wanted a return to peaceful sleep. And that unconsciousness might have been granted if the alien palm hadn't moved slightly in its quest for—God—he hoped not. Herb wanted to be as wrong as bar hopping with a former student and the son of a close family friend. He wanted the shock to end of itself. The line between mentor and pupil should never have been so thoughtlessly crossed.

"Alvin?" Herb whispered. When resolve met with silence, he said again, "Alvin, are you awake?" As a bristly Afro settled onto his chest and the warm body moved, he knew the answer. The tenor voice sent warm breath across his neck, "Your boy hear everything." As Herb felt Alvin's hand reach the cinch of the briefs, he gently removed it, twisted away and sat up on the edge of the bed. His head pounded like a rubber mallet on an airless tire casing. Each thud coursed through him. Then the stiff Afro and a soft cheek settled on his back and arms encircled him. It would be easy to say, "Try it, and your dead," but who was the culprit here, who created this breach, who would be harmed, who violated, who wronged? All Herb could muster was a gentle, "Please, don't." And the shock of that warning came as an abrupt, nervous halt of any advance.

"Please don't be afeared, Mr. Herb. Alvin knows you want what's yours."

"You're wrong."

"Chase off Rufus make you my main man."

How complicated words made this nightmarish irony?

Herb undid the boy's hold and stood. The sheets rustled. Herb clicked on the nightlight. It illuminate a lanky, nude, and aroused youth looking at his main man with the same puppy eyes Herb had for Beth. About to say, "I'm sorry," for being unkind and misleading, he heard a gentle rap on the front door. The recently arrested stalker felt like a dunce in life's corner. A snapshot of this scene would add to Ferringer's case of moral impropriety and be infinitely more difficult to explain to the cops let alone the vice president. If he blamed the situation on whiskey, he'd have to stop drinking forever. A first binge, he thought, and I'm in Gehenna. He wrapped himself in a white terrycloth robe from the closet just as a voice came from the livingroom, "Herb, you okay?"

On his way from the bedroom, he closed the door in time to greet Chris who seemed surprisingly freshened in sandals, jeans, and a midriff-tied, tropical blouse. Dawn outlined the kitchen window and cast light across the tile. Cris flicked on the overhead florescents. Herb's eyes squinched. It was sixish, and she stopped by to check on him before a family outing to the Bahamas on daddy's yacht. Would he like to come? Looking radiant and sharply groomed, she appeared untainted from an almost all-nighter. Two mugs of not so old Blue Mountain made it to the table where the couple sipped and smiled like husband and wife on the morning after. She'd parked his Continental at Tyler's, back of the lot, and gave him the remote and keys. Oh, did he remember Janis Joplin and, God, how spellbound the partygoers were at the Sir John. She thanked him for a memorable night, and asked after Uncle Rufus just as Alvin, dressed in his bell bottoms and sleeveless shirt, came out of the bedroom, took a cup of coffee, and joined them at the table. "Morning got you looking right pretty, Miss Chris," he said.

With confusion transformed to seismic disturbance, she glared at Herb, at his naked chest showing through a loosely tied robe, at disheveled hair, at Alvin picking at a flattened Afro, at the boy's longing gaze, then, mouth agape, averted her stare. "I'd better get out of here."

"Chris—"

She headed for the door, "Please don't foist any explanations on me," and out she went.

Chapter Fifteen

Although he thought Alvin was pissed, Herb knew the matter of the bedroom caper couldn't be glossed over. In the truck on the way to Tyler's for the Continental, they talked about Janis Joplin and Chris going over the top at the Sir John. The delicate rebuke in the bedroom didn't seem to exist, for Alvin believed his prof drove away Uncle Rufus for one reason—Oh, God, I was pissed at the guy's prejudice, Herb wanted to say but thought the talk might turn sour on that line of defense. When Alvin cut off the truck motor in the parking lot, he asked if Herb was angry. There was no sense of remorse, guilt, or self-reproach from the boy. If the young driver wanted, he could blame the pass on drunkenness. But continual smiling glances lessened that easy solution. No excuses. Alvin likely had a juvenile crush on his English Professor. Herb want to suggest masturbation for overcoming the anomaly. Sherry Alley had taught respect to Herb in Junior High, and Tessie Andrews demonstrated that *no* meant *no* in senior high. Masturbation kept him celibate until Beth. What else had he to offer Alvin?

Was Herb a middle ground in the boy's eyes because of the recent breakup with Beth? Did he sense that Chris was merely a stand-in? The youth seemed at home with his come-on because he reached across and placed his hand on Herb's thigh. It was brazen to crawl in bed with your drunk professor, for God's sakes, but a pass in broad daylight? Why did he assume homo-eroticism might please a lovelorn Jewish liberal. Herb slipped out and closed the shotgun door.

This Alvin thing seemed a series of misunderstood, accidental, unintentional, coincidental, yet potentially harmful events. An educator knows that critical moments shape who we become and how well we move on from the unmarked graves of emotional scars. Herb felt his own scars from Mary and then Beth. Of this Herb was sure: he dared not scar Alvin; he appreciated the young man's loyalty; he liked the kid—believed him bright, talented, artistic, socially presentable, potentially successful; he felt empowered by the boy's academic successes; in short, Herb needed to monitor the boy's potential into becoming actual without sexual complications. "Who was drunker last night, Alvin? You or me," he asked.

"I ain't looking for no easy out, Mr. Herb. But thanks."

"I was looking for an easy one, buddy, but—"

"Is a black man too low down for your Coral Gables high society?"

"I'm not pleased with that tag of prejudice. You overstepped the limits of friendship."

"If that be all I get, then, shit, I'll make do for now."

"I appreciate honesty."

"Take a look see inside, and be honest with your own self then."

"Please, let's not become demeaning. I respect you. Please do the same."

"Man, I be giving you more than respect."

"Didn't you invite yourself into my world to become duty-bound?"

"Alvin think he fixing to get a friend when he want more. A man smart as you know my stuff be a gift. Alvin daydreaming us together be good."

"Okay. I think Alvin's talented, bright, charming, more. I feel for you like a brother, like a buddy, like a teacher whoops it up for his stars, his receptors, his proteges. I love the potential in you. I love you but can't make love to you. Does that make sense?"

"Why you fight off Rufus then?"

"Rufus brings people down. What he meant to you was none of my business till that Jew hatred started at the Sir John."

"Look and see what I done to Winnie, to you and Miss Beth, to you and Miss Cris, and last night crawling in bed. Why them things ain't bringing you down?"

"Don't have an answer except maybe some mistakes are mine, not yours, not your intent to bring anyone down.

Sometimes life's downright shitty on its own. Why would we hang out together if either of us caused the other harm?"

"You still my main man, Mr. Herb."

"I respect that. And lucky to be a buddy. Can we keep it that way?"

"You and Miss Beth done brung me out my cocoon, taught me the world got space for black folks."

"You're alright with what I told you?"

"I can wait some."

"When someone compatible comes along, go for it, guy."

"Hey, man, I might get my mind right, and Alvin be hightailing for fine times, but yet and still be a student of old Herb. For sure?" The truck ground a few times and started. Herb backed away. The kid waved as he drove off. The morning was bright and the sun warmed Herb's shoulders. Sometimes the weather seemed right for diverting storms.

Chapter Sixteen

Chris decided that she understood about Herb and Alvin, and *yes* she'd be happy to legitimize the English prof by going with him to hear Ira Sullivan. She apologized in advance, though, for any rendezvous that might occur, after which, of course, he'd be on his own. And, by the way, she didn't at all mind if Alvin tagged along. He was a great guy. "I'm so, so grateful for Janis Joplin."

Herb needed friendship as well as her company. He felt like a born again virgin anyway, and a rather unattached one to boot. At home, he obsessed about Beth and devised ways to jump-start the relationship. Scenario after scenario after scenario. Peace escaped him. Sleep escaped him. Anguish and frustration didn't. And the masturbation nearly recommended to Alvin, provided fleeting suppression for Herb. Judge Snowden's restraining order kept him, though, from the presence of his beloved. And the good Doctor Shockett wouldn't hesitate to enforce it. Exercise at the gym and teaching served as therapy. Chris kept him from becoming a social recluse. Cultural events, weekend activities, and bar hopping with her served as therapy.

Although the English Department hired a young, gorgeous adjunct, he felt loathe to make a move but indulged in casual conversations at the faculty lounge, the student union, the corridors of higher learning, or anywhere else the young woman started one. Her talk mainly centered around teaching for she knew about his nomination for professor of the year. The flattery made him feel useful but wanting to date worried him. Anyone new in his life might change the love scoreboard—girlfriends, five, Herb, zero. And it wasn't fair to expect the girl to accept second fiddle to Beth's first chair. The new female had a nice name, too: Lorraine Shore. Would a sixth botch affect a job he loved as well as unhinge him further?

Anyway, Friday night he and Chris, the greatest standby a guy could want, went together, as if on a real date, in his rehabilitated Continental. He picked her up at the family's Rivera Drive, immodest home. She insisted he meet her parents, and inside the home formal introductions occurred with Doctor and Mommy Curry. The dainty cross on mommy's neck chain made him uneasy from the outset. Chris's parents were too smiley, too formal for the casual tastes of a free spirit. In the living room, Herb stood by A New Century Bible the size of an unabridged dictionary. After hellos and handshakes, the Curry's went for the prepared, gentleman-caller goodies. Herb read verse two of *Corinthians* from the pedestaled new testament beside the grand piano. "If I have the gift of Prophecy and can fathom all mysteries and all knowledge, and if I have a faith that can move mountains, but have not love, I am nothing." A two-by-four between the eyes. Did God or the Currys display that passage?

At home in a museum, daddy wore a dapper blue suit and tie as if he were about to address a congregation with a sermon for the day. Mommy looked ready for opera at the Met in a black three-quarter gown with no neckline to enhance that dainty diamond studded cross resting on her satin-protected chest. They appeared as Christian as Mary's folks that ill-fated day in Minnesota. To say that Herb felt out of place in his shirt sleeves, vest, and bell bottom dungarees was a sure starter for a fashion conversation he hoped would not happen tonight. Thoughtful chit-chat started in the lush, old-fashioned living room among ancestral portraits, alabaster statuettes, French provincial antiques, and a glass menagerie-adorned fireplace mantle above which hung an emperor-sized oil of the family patriarch. Cordials and evaluations happened before Chrissy was free to accept company. Did daddy and mommy wish to inspect his circumcised dick?

Caviar and quiche canapés indulged in, the couple bid the Currys adieu. Chris sat beside him on the front seat as they drove down a circular drive amid lighted poincianas, banyans, and red and gold Xora hedges while mommy and daddy waved from the porch of Tara: the scene was cinematic. One hand on the wheel and the other on the girl beside him. After the kelly green impression of the home, Chris's orange furniture and mid-wife's chair above Maury's Garage, he believed, mocked her parents—God, she seemed so much more real. Both had been pleasant to him, the chit-chat rather engaging and literary, and not at all meddlesome. He begrudgingly liked them. Soon Herb would learn how misleading first impressions could be, how blind he was to his own prejudices, and how much he needed to gain trust in older *goyim*. Not all of them were missionary freaks or Jew haters like Lola May Ferringer, Mary's parents, or Uncle Rufus.

Something about Herb represented a safe cover for Chris. Catering to her wishes certainly trained him in the social graces of Coral Gables society of which Alvin had spoken so condescendingly. The same society for which Lola May Ferringer thought him poisonous. But what the hell, gentlemanly training never hurt any kike crossing clannish boundaries. Beside the continuance of a strong friendship, Herb legitimized the single-but-trying music professor in doctor daddy's eyes for, later on, invitations came along to be her beau on the yacht, at country club dinners, box seats with the family at Dade County opera, Grove theater, symphony orchestra concerts. Actually, Herb had been dead wrong about the Currys. They were tolerant, progressive, community minded sorts. And his selection as an escort for daughter until she found what she really sought, or until he did, was a decision her parents trusted.

At the Coconut Grove night spot, Sullivan was his usual eclectic, multi-faceted self. Herb served as a genteel phoney leaving Chris at the first sign of any interested gentleman and returning only upon request. He danced with her. Asked other girls to dance with good results, but abandoned those good results if Chris needed him. He nursed one drink and not Southern Comfort because one hangover clouding his self-esteem squelched any desire for so horrendous a repeat. In short, he had a passable time enjoying jazz and socializing between sets until the unimaginable happened, a turn of events, a quake to his equilibrium. The beloved Shockett—Beth in full diaphanous array—appeared with an ersatz companion, the interim department head. The good ex-husband must have been at a medical convention or something of the like, and she'd gotten permission for a night on the town. Or maybe she was after some additional getting even. As they seated themselves across the club, Herb decided that he and Chris needed to be up and clutching each other on the dance floor, to be intimate, and compelled to sway and hug. Chris asked that if the dance was not for Alvin's benefit, who was it for then? "Indulge me," was all Herb said. To the Penguins recording of "Earth Angel," they wrapped around each other like jelly in a cake roll. And on they went. Only after "Wooley Bully," Mamma Cass singing, "Monday, Monday," and Marvin Gaye's, "Heard It Through the Grapevine," did the floor clear for Sullivan's next set, and the newfound Arthur and Katherine Murray, hand in hand, returned to their table. Chris wanted to know why Herb sat with his back to the stage. Sorry was all the excuse he gave and pulled out his former seat for her. When the stage lit up and the room dimmed, he ducked out to the bathroom.

At the urinal, he barely got it put back into his fly when he felt a familiar presence behind him. Herb closed his eyes. Is it breathing patterns we hear, the rustle of familiar clothing, a change of temperature from another's nearby body heat, the scent of identifiable flesh that names the unseen? Is it some unknowable aura we feel obliged to sensate through, an aura that foreshadows coming experiences? From the fragrance of Tabu Perfume, he knew instantly who wore it, but nervousness, anxiety, confusion, palpitations kept him against the white porcelain as if violating some universal law forced him to hide. When soft, warm, delightful lips rested on his neck, it was time to see, to hold, to love what had once ended in emotional bankruptcy. She wore one of her seductive, diaphanous frocks and a pearl neckless. Her stilettos clicked on the tiles of his heart as she moved to pull him into a stall, and without any greeting, planted herself on him like that first kiss in a hidden bower off the driveway at the University Faculty Club. Hardly time for a purr, a breathless, "I've missed you so," Beth's lips met his, their tongues reached for unreserved passion, his pants slipped to the floor, she sat him on the commode, raised her dress, and wrapped herself around the hard pulse of his being. How unreal this elating scene played, how erotic, how mesmerizing, how orgiastic. Was the harmony he heard overflowing from Sullivan's quintet or was it the lustful melody hotly rising from a lonely heart, now a rejuvenated one, and reverberating through him? Then just as he felt beneath the table at the Sir John Club, he became encircle by and immersed in a frenzied amusement park, whirled on a carousel of emotions, rambled through a fairground of rebirth. How was it possible after separation, this resumption came as natural, as real, as intense as an unsurpassed night in Key West before, before, before. Life before, love before, hope before, and now his soul spun on a turn of events as supernatural as Beth's disappearance from his life, his arms, from his ecstasy, from his need, and from this stall where he sat fully clothed, sat slumped helplessly forward on a toilet seat, face in hands, sat and wept for a return of sanity.

How ever long the crying jag lasted, it nailed embarrassment, humility, and self-deprecation like a *condemned* sign on an unsound building. He tried to regain composure, tried to subdue childish whimpering, tried to relocate the man who disappeared along with his fantasy. Then a sheepish baritone from the next stall inquired, "You all right in there?" and his "Yeah," seemed to satisfy any concern. "Thanks for asking," he said in stead of opening with, "I'm falling apart because of a demented female." Strangely, it would have mellowed him if Alvin sat in the next stall. Strangely, he felt the need for a friend, some masculine presence, familiar and supportive, to tell his story of "Herb and Beth" from his perspective. Another male needed to listen to guts being spilled, nod sympathetically, and curse the bitch at appropriate points in the tale. His father's ashes lay in the earth above a tomb where Herb buried them one dark, illegal midnight, so there wasn't any parental wisdom to rely on. And what Sol might have to say about love would be surprisingly akin to what his son already knew. Love torments body and mind like an overdose and mostly you struggle to survive it.

He splashed water on his face, dabbed it with a paper towel, and vacated the bathroom before any stall buddy had a chance to face his humbled, humiliated shit-house mate. Back at the table, Chris sat alone. Sullivan had finished his last set. Herb paid for the drinks, and they took off as Fats Domino taunted with, "I found my thrill on Blueberry Hill." Beside him once again in the Continental, Chris sensed disquiet, but hadn't the relentless tools to draw him out. For her, his mood squelched any opportunity to launch a conversation about who's who this week, to explicate a most recent charitable project, to talk about music history or sight reading, to issue opinions about discrimination, the medical profession, her awards and accolades, to excuse a doctorate in music instead of medicine, or to recount details of growing up among the privileged in Coral Gables. Other than her, "You're unusually quiet," to penetrate his private anguish, she remained silent. He wondered if Alvin sat beside him, the "telling" which was willing to begin now would, in fact, offend a dancer who treasured a painting which testified to his worthiness as a de-ghettoized human. Herb had nothing to offer the quiet ride back to Rivera Drive. Perhaps misery is a state our souls must endure in silence.

Chris asked him to park at the head of her parents' driveway, and when he cut the engine, they sat like riders on a New York subway. When she pecked him on a cheek, he felt words breathed into his ear, "It's a shame because as guys go, you're a class *A* gentleman." He was too busy beating himself up internally with another rehash of Key West to register such praise. Once again on the verge of a demeaning crying jag, he reached for the ignition thinking to get to Tara's door before, before, before. A gentle hand stopped him from seeking the solitude he required. Perhaps he'd seek psychological help come Monday. Find out why the edge seemed so close of late. And in desperation, he bit hard on his bottom lip.

Chris brought her agenda to a head by placing an ear against his chest as if the emotional heaves might be on the embarrassment forecast. Holding his breath lest she brand him a bonafide sissy, he felt her hand on his crotch. She began a gentle but deliberate massage to confirm his deviant sexual preference. Harve de Grace's small road sign began to enlarge as the distance narrowed on the highway of pleasure. Was she surprised? She expected indifference from a female's intervention. But on she went until obviously and unmistakably the gentleman didn't suffer from erectile dysfunction in her presence. How confused she must have felt now what with that failure above Maury's Garage as proof of impotence. Yet slowly his zipper came down, and the road sign stood in full, sound structural view from the center of a grassy swale to symbolize a legitimate township. She twisted it slightly, he guessed, to be sure its stiffness wasn't half-hearted.

Would daddy come from behind Tara's hedges and have him arrested on the spot for being a complicitous recipient? Did Dr. Curry store a riffle with ammunition in his game room? Could passiveness be used as a defense for *sex with a socialite* in front of her father's magistrate friend? His not so little guy stood proud now that he'd been brought from hiding. And he wasn't at all interested in crying. Herb's hips began to raise from the leather seat, and his mind quit its psychological bashing. What harm if his arm found its way around her or his palm urged the back of her head. What she said before working on him was, "I'll help you discover proper sexuality." And, by God, he was amenable to the conversion.

Chapter Seventeen

Herb originated a new course called "Issues in Social Drama" which filled and closed shortly after second semester registration began. Dean Alvarez gave it an upper level designation after he saw the syllabus and prerequisites. Its description included Ibsen, Becket, Brecht, Hellman, and Shaw, and was recommended for English majors. A dean's list student, a dancer, a singer, a student of dramaturgy strode into the classroom, row one, seat one, giving the young prof calling roll a white toothed smile amid Harry Belafonte features. Having acquiesced to the Suntan U. image, Alvin wore black Bermuda shorts and a lean tank top, muscles displayed as advertisements, and wraparound shades like Boss Man in *Cool Hand Luke*. Except for a caramel complexion, he blended with other rubber thonged dudes who didn't win nearly the notice from big-haired, mini-skirted girls in the class.

Before semester registration opened, Alvin, and Chris sat with him at the Sir John Club for Jimmy Reed and the Memphis Blues show. Taking Herb's advanced class never came up. His buddy got Chris's signature to override a closed class, to maximize Alvin's chances of getting in without having to bug the instructor, and to sidestep prerequisite requirements. Did his buddy think Herb would keep a talented student from drama study because of informality unbecoming professional decorum? God, Herb even jargonized like Lola May who recently parlayed a promotion to Associate Vice President and seemed destined for Dr. Beaumont's job upon his retirement. The President's health, of late, loomed ominously over his tenure.

No doubt Arts and Sciences as well as English were top of Ferringer's agenda for renovation. Her mossgrown ideas of curriculum bordered on reactionary. To boot, the former English Department Head decided not to return, so Dean Max Alvarez made sounds as if Herb were in contention for the position. What a clash of educational ideology his leadership would pose for a President like Ferringer. How would she ever keep his staff out of the language lab? The School of Music—particularly friends like Dean Bitter, Professor Kraushaar, and Professor Curry—gave strong vocal support at informal faculty chitchat. President of the Faculty Council also felt inclined toward a man voted teacher of the year by students and colleagues. The only sure negative vote would have been Beth Shockett, Professor of American Lit and newly married to her former husband. Ironically, Herb had gotten an invitation to the small ceremony at Temple Beth David in the Rhodes section of Miami, but thought that being in attendance might violate a restraining order which the newly-re-weds forgot to send along with their magisterial-looking, embossed invitation. Anyway, Herb took the invite as a notice of termination, request for a gift, and, indeed, sent the couple a reel to reel, portable video recorder and a copy of Francisco Zefferilli's *Romeo and Juliet* as a gift in lieu of his presence.

Herb's love life certainly qualified him to teach drama, and he'd become well schooled in social issues before and after that night in Dade County Jail. And here he was before a group of eager minds, some of whom were from Freshman Composition, who like Alvin, got around the prerequisite requirements. The educational challenge was stimulating. He'd start strong so that anyone wanting to drop within the allotted window had ample time.

The black Romeo in row one, seat one, had officially accepted salary for office work enabling him to quit long hours and minimum wages as a Steven's Market stock boy and devote time to community theater. Just as he danced into "Issues in Social Drama," Alvin brought the house down in a summer stock musical review at Overtown's Lyceum Theater. Herb video taped highlights of songs and dances, "Wild Women Don't Have the Blues," and "I Guess I'm Just a Lucky So and So," Alvin's stylized performance before an enraptured audience. When Alvin neared graduation, Herb'd send video clips to agents and practitioners in New York,

Chicago, and L.A. as well as local dramaturges with a well crafted cover letter, "—raw talent and primal energy of Miami's best talent." Both Jerry Herman and Bob Fosse would respond with hand written encouragements. Frankel Productions would assign a scout to keep abreast of Alvin's work. Herb arranged an audition with the artistic director at *The Playhouse* on Miami Beach for a world premier musical called "Juke Box Jangles." In his senior year, Alvin landed the lead, a Bo Jangles character later to be energized by Ben Vareen once it played off Broadway for a moderate run into obscurity. The skid row expressionist musical would take Alvin, after graduation, to the Great White Way as an understudy and an assistant choreographer. "Juke Box Jangles" became the kid's first step to establishing his own dance company in Harlem and a lifelong dream for both Alvin and his mother who became business manager. But Alvin McKinnon's future was a story for another venue while his mentor and friend faced the dire prospect of Lola May Ferringer becoming President of the University of Miami.

Faculty and staff attending Dr. Beaumont's annual *newcomers banquet* fully expected the President to announce his retirement and name Miss Lola May Ferringer as interim head of the university. The event catered to an overflow crowd which required patio dinning to accommodate almost three-hundred sad revelers, sad at least from perspectives likened to Herb's and Dean Alvarez's; namely, a progressive one. Conservatives and traditionalists would be elated once the announcement came. Under Ferringer, campus police and security stood to gain budgetary ground because, according to Ferringer, the university needed a full scale crackdown on perverts, queers, and liberals. Foreign Language, Engineering, Business, Math, and Theology stood to pull off a coup while the Fine Arts and Letters folks watched graves being dug. The sciences and medicine straddled the fence or were too immersed in research and grant money to care about campus politics. The Education Faculty required opinionated attorneys to tell them where to stand, but the law school vacillated. They leaned away from Ferringer because she was female although she qualified as a skirt who earmarked funding for their favorite programs. Being a woman was the sole criteria Physical Education needed for a blackball. The Ferringer *in-favor-set* came to the Faculty Club in unusually high numbers to support a crackdown on the Suntan U. image, frills and arty nonsense in the curriculum, moral impropriety among students and faculty, budgetary excesses, frat houses, itinerant experts' programs, and women in men's sports. They supported President Nixon, our military sacrifices to stem Communism, and good, old American family and religious values.

When Dr. Beaumont delivered his address, the relief of progressives around the room became infinitely more palpable than the despondence of conservatives who got it straight from the dias, "I thank the well-wishers who fill the halls of this great university. The oncologist reported a new lease on my life for me. All biopsies negative." Applause rang out spontaneously. "Your president," Beaumont continued, "is as strong and sound as a hurricane in August." Lola May's following presentation of his gold, retirement watch transformed into a heartfelt congratulations and a memento of his seventh year of leadership and service. Ferringer told the president that his faculty and staff wished seven and more years for a man so loved by his colleagues and the greater Miami community—to which the associate vice-president brought the house to their feet. Desert came and dancing commenced.

Herb excused himself from the seat beside Dean Alvarez and made his way through the crowd to the driveway. It was a muggy, tropical night with little breeze, the type that kept you bobbing in the middle of the Gulfstream on a sloop headed for Bimini or Nassau. It was stuffier inside with the overburdened air conditioning than in the outside humidity. For old time's sake, he found a bench near a secluded bower where beginnings had once been fresh and exciting. His suede blazer came off and laid itself on the back of the seat. His tie let his collar loose as arms stretched across the back rail. All in all he felt pleased with his first year as an English professor. Certainly a year of traumatic events with the loss of a father he treasured and a woman who, like Janis Joplin, lived inside her song and aimed directly for raw veins. Yet he survived the overdose, perhaps not without help, but nonetheless he remained creative and productive. He owed a great deal to one Liberty City kid who stood by his main man like a worried brother. He owed a great deal to Chris who waved pom poms at the foot of his bleachers and cheered for a win. Yes, the world was a good place with good people who cared unselfishly for one another. There is a God, he thought, a primal force flowing through existence just as the poet Shelley saw it. Like water coursing into eddies in a river bank, goodness flowed through men who need only receive it. It ran through Ferringers, through Rufuses, through Shocketts, through unsympathetic police and restraining order judges, and the stars tonight testified to its universality. Herb knew in his heart and soul that nothingness, endings, terminations, hatred, and politics bore threads of Good weaving them together with love, friendship, charity, kindness, and honorable deeds into a tapestry that hung magnificently on a cosmos above the Deity's mantle. Within a similar glow of faith, his dad's legacy threaded its way into a son's life to face tomorrows and other tomorrows after that.

When his eyes opened, he found Beth Shockett at the far end of his bench. So cat like an arrival, not a leaf rustled, not one footfall sent a clue, not a slat betrayed her alighting, not a twitch or sound interrupted his notion of being alone. Yet she alighted on the edge of the bench, knees clasped together, hands folded in her lap. Surprised by so stealthy a coming, he knew for certain this presence was no apparition, no sissy-like head game, no bout with fantasy. For what seemed a re-tightening of time's unbound story, neither spoke. The words and music of *Unchained Melody* drifted from the party inside to where Herb and Beth sat sculpted in seclusion, forged by expectancy less than a bench apart. The song hadn't nudged his mind until it reached an ironic crescendo at the phrase, " . . . At last we're face to face . . . ." Then to qualify *Unchained Melody*, she said softly, "I'm sorry." And went on, "Really, really sorry."

"Wasn't it Eric Segal who said, 'Love means never having to say you're sorry?'"

"He was wrong," she said.

"Should one think, then, that love torments us like a drug overdose and mostly body and mind struggle to survive it."

"Have you survived me?"

"Must you have an answer?"

"Only if you wish."

"Why are you here? I don't mean on this earth or this campus, but on this bench?"

"To even the playing field."

"Ah. You heard the department head rumor."

"I love my job as much as you."

"Jeez."

"You're upset."

"First off, Ferringer wouldn't allow a Jew a powerful position at her university."

"What about your friend Dean Alvarez?"

"Tonight, Dr. Beaumont's health almost retired Max. Ferringer doesn't cater to Jews. Second, it pisses me that she thinks of me as spiteful, small minded, and unprofessional."

"Isn't that how men are?"

"What about your restraining order?"

"It's expired."

"So then, the playing field is equal again."

"Seems that way."

"Does Dr. Shockett know you're unbalance it?"

"I really did love you. Still do."

"I try to un-believe that. Yet crossing this line you set in Key West was intimately harmful. You forced me into the shadows then to quit."

"Now it's you who's upsetting. Why think I would hurt you?"

"Because you can."

"Well then, my effort to renew things is undesired."

"You knew damn well it wasn't before following me here."

"Am I still so disarming?"

"God."

"In our next lives, we'll have unsullied chances."

"Wonder how often you'll dream of me till then?"

"Would it please you if I said often?"

"Well then, I'll live on in twilight."

"You'd know my suffering if I kissed you goodbye."

"I'm not well healed from our last kiss."

Naturally his intimation in no way stopped Beth Shockett from gliding above him, rustling like wind though a luffed sail, planting her warm, supple lips on his, and staying on course as he fought hidden, erogenous waves of emotion. Charmingly, she blew off the sanctity of her recent marriage, a shoal skirted as if she were re-divorced. Defiantly, he remained floundering and motionless on a secret wooden dock outside a naive banquet room where Dr. Shockett believed in her phoney trip to the ladies' room. Defiantly, he acted out his initial, casual stance as if arms spread eagle on a back rail, eyes closed, legs apart, hips forward, back curved in a former relaxed privacy had maintained their substance. Herb's resting arms obeyed him, his legs passed an urge to wrap around her, his breath observed tranquility, his shoulder and back muscles remained at ease, and any facial giveaways were blank. Yet a self-destructive nether dweller slowly began a betrayal of his once strong comrades' now sabotaged pretense of indifference. He cared if she witnessed his peter's treason. The talebearer confirmed what she already knew. If cool reactions send a definitive message, his relaxed body with one rising renegade persisted beyond the siren withdrawing her tantalizing lips from their mark. A hasty glimpse down brought a smile to that moist, un-reddened mouth and walking off in a swish of diaphanous material, Beth said, "Oh, how perfectly flattering, Herb."

Chapter Eighteen

Herb learned from talks at the doctor's home that Geoffrey Curry harbored progressive leanings. Although relocating to the suburbs when eminent domain took half his yard, the patriarch maintained participation in The First United Methodist Church of Miami, a progressive bastion among changing inner city neighborhoods. He donated liberally to the religious institution and to the arts and fine arts education which marked his Coral Gables home for gatherings of Miami's intellectuals and societal leaders. Herb needed support for a new program that had the ears of Dean Alvarez and President Beaumont. He openly asked Chris's dad for a hand.

The doctor invited Herb to a Mensa meeting at the Riviera estate. The Mensa people in attendance included influential people like Dean Jonathan Bitter, Rabbi Len Kaplan of Temple E-Manuel, Pastor Roeby Williamson of the First Baptist Church of Miami, President, Sister Mary Olanga of Barry University, Serene Hester of the School Board, and others with whom Herb wished to network.

The meeting focused on the University of Miami and its educational leadership in South Florida. Dr. Beaumont, the keynote speaker, highlighted engineering, law, medicine, theater, and music as benchmarks of excellence in Florida and nationwide. As the official, but unannounced new department head for English, Herb had been asked to facilitate an informal give-and-take on education. But the new program, the seeds of which germinated while Herb attended Columbia, had a chance for fruition with support from the community. The English curriculum lacked accessibility for too many students not only at Miami but on other campuses. He felt that students were not powerfully served by elitist pedagogy. As the weaker students graduated public schools, it became clear that flunking them out of the Freshman classes wasn't an answer.

English needed to survive its mounting failure rate and

embattled standards. He was convinced that auditorium lectures, the grading system, and outmoded teaching strategies were among the culprits. This evening at the Curry's seemed a two Manhattan challenge where he found it unsettling to break away from the warm camaraderie of Dean Max Alvarez into a sea of strangers. But breakaway he did into a discussion between The First Baptist Church and The School Board.

Mrs. Hester, a short, slender, fortyish woman with penetrating hazel eyes, turned to acknowledge Herb in mid sentence, "Join in, Mr. Rizer. As I was saying, reverend, rapid changes in our demographics affect the school board as well." She might have been a light-skinned Negro but for her gently waving, jet-black hair that brushed the shoulders of a pink blazer. She was an Iranian who married Dade Savings and Loan Association. The man to whom she spoke, a black-suited guy with one platform shoe, seemed paused in thought.

Roeby Williamson spoke with a Miami accent—light Southern with a tinge of Northeast, ending *r's* dropped and overdone vowel sounds—"Never before in Miami—and I'm a native, my dear Mrs. Hester—have I thought it unwise to leave keys in the ignition or lock my front door or hire security for our church. That is a radical change from the provincial Miami of the past," he said. His auburn crewcut showed a hint of gray in its sideburns, and Herb guessed the minister's freckled, ashen features to be mid-thirties.

Mrs. Hester spoke with a musical lilt. "Yet Dade County's residents, Allah be praised, have not resisted the greatest change of our time, integration," she said.

The minister's deep, pastoral tone carried an edge of dismay. "Not resisted but fled."

Serene Hester took Herb by the arm. "Yes, reverend, we're a city in shock. What, though, will stabilize our tropical paradise?"

"I'm stymied," the minister said. "A few years ago my congregation was less than fifteen percent minority. Then, fifty-fifty. Now I preach to an Afro-American congregation with a small white minority." He raised his chin and loosened his collar.

When Herb moved to New York City, Dade County had been segregated—The Shores, North Miami, South Miami Heights, Miami, Curtis Park, Allapatah, among other municipalities were lily white while Overtown, Liberty City, Lemon City, Richmond Heights, West Coconut Grove were the recognized, black communities. When he returned, white flight was on the rampage. Windward, the downtown neighborhood around The First Baptist Church, had become, in fact, Afro-American inside of two years. Herb had witnessed the change when he visited a black childhood friend.

Herb's buddy was a kid who lived in a post-civil war log cabin on a land grant made to his grandfather, a former slave. Although Daniel Lee's parents worked for the Rizer's, his mama never dined at the Rizer table nor would she let her son do so. The only times the kids broke bread together was when Herb got a driver's license and the two buddies integrated Trail Drugs' Luncheonette during a time when national turmoil seemed to bypass sleepy, provincial Miami. As a child, Herb was oblivious to Daniel Lee's skin color so racial divides never entered his thinking. Yet through Daniel Lee's parents, Herb saw his own skin as a derogatory condition—The Man, honky, ofay, white trash, home boy. "Child, you don't act white," Daniel Lee's mama would say. "No white boy eats Colored favorites like you," his pap had admonished as Herb, uninvited to the dinner table, always ate separately from the black family. In and around the log cabin where, as kids, they hung out, he heard the litany of race separation. So it was natural for Herb to ask Minister Williamson, "And the difference in your church now, is it anything other than skin color?"

The minister continued, "I feel like an outsider in my congregation and look for a way in."

The same rang true of Herb's childhood experiences with Daniel Lee. *Schvartz* was how Minnie referred to Daniel Lee and his parents and voiced her stereotypic generalities as freely as Mr. and Mrs. Lee—honkeys, The Man. "May I suggest there's clannishness on both sides of the racial divide," Herb said.

The minister fingered a cross which hung around his neck. "They're good Christians just like my former congregation. I'm the one having difficulty with the changes."

If Mensa members needed a picture of prejudice, he'd damn well better forget the niceties of social gatherings and draw one. "Bigots fight integration, propagate the racial divide on both sides of the cultural lines drawn at America's beginnings," Herb said.

"You can not believe my flock harbors such prejudice," the reverend said.

"I learned as a child that biases haven't any cultural boundaries."

Frowning now, Roeby Williamson said, "So I'm to believe that from my new Godfearing congregation, I'm isolated. My white face causes discontent. Yet my Negroes come to services, support church functions, and don't go elsewhere for their spiritual needs."

"How many Blacks are in the church's administration? On the board of directors? What committees do they head?"

"None. But we included them in all church activities."

Serene Hester's school board perspective seemed similar. "If you are hinting at a put-yourself-in-their-place scenario, Mr. Rizer, it does not enlighten the socialization problem," she said. "Integrating the schools works rather poorly because of white flight. White teachers at schools like Miami Jackson and Miami Edison, nearly all black student bodies now, feel set apart like Minister Williamson, isolated like whites who remain in changed neighborhoods. Why won't Negroes reach out with a helping hand?"

"From another perspective, ma'am, Blacks struggled with that Southern fist around a hangman's noose with few white helping hands. These Miamians cry for relatives who were lynched, cousins who were beaten, a national leader who was shot on a balcony in Atlanta. There is anger and prejudice in their ghetto where they live in a violent, negative environment. As assimilation continues, tolerance and understanding will thrive on both sides of the divide."

"That violence is behind us, thank God," said the minister, "and Christians continue to preach brotherhood in the Lord and peace among men."

Herb couldn't let the last remark stand unchallenged. "I don't think The Nation of Islam agrees, reverend. Perhaps Jesse Jackson's boycotts, economic sanctions, and King's passivist pro-action will prove the Black Muslims wrong. Miami isn't immune to the voices of Malcolm X, Louis Farrahkan, Angela Davis, Stokley Carmichael, or Huey Newton."

"Perhaps not, Mr. Rizer, perhaps not," conceded Roeby Williamson.

Serene Hester shook her head, and eyes downcast, arm in arm, she escorted Herb toward the lectern in front of the fireplace. He felt a tinge of nervousness. Herb accepted an introduction from Dr. Curry. He caught a high-sign from Chris who peeked in from the foyer. The joke he told got healthy laughter. He asked the group to brainstorm techniques teachers used to motivate them. During the audience's thoughtful hesitancy, he went on, "think of a personal mentor and tell us what techniques he or she employed to help you achieve your goals—and I think we've got a room full of achievers."

"Over achievers," someone called followed by laughter.

Max Alvarez offered, "My most memorable mentor taught by example. He showed me that compassion is action not condition." Jonathan Bitter added that he'd been motivated with stern discipline, a firm but fair hand. Mrs. Beaumont offered that personal attention inspired her. A caring teacher was paramount to her learning. Another woman volunteered that thought provoking lectures moved her. "Whatever inspired you, it is the prime objective of the school to create an atmosphere where mentor's flourish,"

Herb said. "Studies show, and I'll share the sources with you shortly, that in educational organizations, inclusion of practitioners, teachers, if you will, in the decision-making process increases commitment and productivity. It enfranchises talent. It releases potential. Too many educational institutions are built by architects who have never worked inside a classroom. Might those who have, shed important light on a plant's physical needs? Who designs rooms which echo so badly that hearing one another is a problem? Who buys inflexible furniture to inflict conformity? Who designs auditoriums without adjacent restrooms or ones with too few stalls to accommodate women? Who builds massive, wasted hallway space, who cannot imagine anything other than rectangular learning space, and so on? But more important, who designs a curriculum on the premise that all learners must progress, lock step, together or fail?"

Herb cited Peter Drucker and his work with General Motors where workers, both menial and creative, knew more about challenges facing the company than top management. An interesting and spirited discussion ensued among the Mensa members about Drucker's theories, not unfamiliar to them, and Drucker's organizational development, a factor in Herb's staffing model, a key to his new program at the university.

"Hospitals must empower doctors; precincts listen to rank and file policemen; industry depends on workers' involvement; schools must be run by faculties; and, yes, prisons—in a more limited sense—should seek advice from inmates," Herb said. An eerie silence followed. These community leaders lived with decisions made from the pinnacle of a hierarchy to which they had ascended, a ladder of power they had perpetrated in deference to a man or woman who once stood, before their ascension, on the top rung. To abdicate that power was unwieldy, revolutionary, progressive. His presentation was far from over when it concluded because the question and answer session eventually broke into small groups of supporters, skeptics, and opponents. Herb went from group to group nurturing one and with the others, fielding objections with studies, experts' opinions, books, examples of institutions where differentiated staffing thrived. That the interaction lasted well past one in the morning was a tribute to the evening's spirited discourse. All in all, the university leadership was impressed and won over with the support and affirmation from the community leaders. Skepticism dwindled. The opponents left. In the end, several heavy duty contributors pledged financial commitments to Herb's proposal including Dr. Curry. On the way out, Dr. Beaumont patted Herb on the back. "Good job," he said.

As Beth Shockett suspected, Dean Alvarez named Herb head of the English faculty. If he adhered to his own staffing proposals, the position had to be open to review and selected by a faculty vote. The university president and dean of arts and sciences were reluctant to abdicate their decision making power, but Herb prevailed in that regard and was selected by his colleagues. With the support of Dr. Curry and Mensa, Beaumont and Alvarez were primed for innovative change.

When Herb's grant for differentiated staffing came through, a fine arts college within the university became reality. It functioned seamlessly during the term of a three year grant. Teaching facilitators responsible for day to day operations of the program were selected by faculty vote. Beaumont inserted a caveat that their resolutions be subject to his review. In exchange, Herb got President Beaumont, Deans Alvarez and Bitter, and other administrators to teach a course in the new fine arts college. Differentiated staffing was underway. A system of evaluations instead of grades was underway. Open labs and flex time came into being. Individualized instruction happened. U of M received state wide notability for initiating Black Studies, Women's Studies, Learning Labs, a two week course shopping window for students, interdisciplinary team teaching, and a system for matching learning and teaching styles. Educators from

Wisconsin, Perdue, Northwestern, Rutgers, NYU, Berkley and others sent observers who returned to their universities to implement what they observed and liked. These programs received word-of-mouth and journal recognition before their demise during the reign of Lola May Ferringer as university president. Once the grant money dried up, she wounded the fine arts college by standing firmly against it. She withheld funds and demoted, reassigned, retired, or fired proponents. Yet Herb gave the Associate Vice-President ideological palpitations during his rapid ascendency on a ladder she hoped fervently to topple.

Chapter Nineteen

Professional advancement did not satisfy the need for companionship of a head facilitator in his mid twenties. Since campus leadership now demanded time, Herb immersed himself beyond sane hours. It kept his mind off of a failed love life. Without company on weekends, he'd drive to Merritt Island, Key West, Avon Park, Sebring or other Florida remote destinations to burn leisure time. Spook Hill, one of his favorites, had nothing there including crowds. He'd check into a motel or if none available, stay in the Continental at a wayside, write in his diary or read until sleep or morning came. He'd tour Mt. Dora subconsciously awaiting a love-clone to join him at breakfast, to suggest buying this or that souvenir, to bump into him on a sidewalk or in a doorway, or to sit beside him in a theater. The more recluse, the more haunted he became. On campus, he sensed rushes of inexplicable exhilaration and tension when Beth Shockett appeared in a corridor, at the student union, at any campus commons, or at meetings within the department. Many times he'd fantasize encounters in a broom closet, an empty classroom, a meter room, between remote stacks at the library, or any cubbyhole where renewal seemed plausible. Recovery from those fantasies had a rawness inside that needed time and antacids. At home, privacy merely fed sore dreams. Yet he never avoided Beth. He decided to desensitize himself. But his efforts hardly worked.

With colleagues, Herb became brusque when they criticized Beth. Was it her smugness, sense of superiority, or his overcompensation that wagged tongues in the English department? They thought she shirked duties. On one occasion, Herb learned that she cancelled a class. In a humanities course, her team professor sounded off about being strapped with all the paperwork and evaluations as well as extra teaching duty. Were the complaints merely professional jealousy because the department facilitator favored Mrs. American Lit?

Herb socialized solely with Chris Curry. She was a glamorous, comfortable sidekick whose self-worth needed support from a companion of diplomatic standing at the university. She lessened his desire to place Miami in a rear view mirror. As they became inseparable, each enjoyed the other's company at clubs, theater, cinema, opera, and also the water activities Dade County offered. On skis behind Dr. Curry's speedboat, they performed like professionals at Cypress Gardens. Favorite dining spots like *The Garden Restaurant* and *Court of Two Dragons* at Sonesta Beach often preceded outings. Alvin kept them abreast of shows at the Sir John such as a chance to hear Satchmo Armstrong and Pete Fountain. Yet other than goodnight kisses, hugs, and a great deal of hand holding, Chris ultimately resigned herself to Herb's hots for the same sex. After all, she was a beautiful woman, not only in her own eyes but also in his, and his sexual apathy became insulting if he were straight. Since Alvin hadn't found a significant other, he tagged along regularly. Yet the trio balanced well within their circular lack of interest in complications until they sailed on a bare boat charter during Spring break to the Bahamas.

Holding a captain's certification from the Coast Guard, Herb secured a magnificent Choy Lee, blue water equipped, for the vacation intercession. Along with Chris, also a competent sailor, he planned a Gulfstream crossing to Bimini then on to Cat Cay, Chub Cay, Nassau, Andros, and back to Miami. Alvin insisted, since he knew nothing about boats and oceans, on taking charge of the kitchen which he learned to call the galley. The threesome departed late afternoon from Dinner Key in Coconut Grove with the idea of anchoring off Bimini for a day of fun on a stark white, isolated beach with crystalline waters. Just before daybreak, they anchored and slept until mid morning, then ate, fished, scuba dove, and explored the shell-laden sand and dunes and underbrush. Alvin, like a native in cut offs with splotches of salt where the ocean evaporated from his toffy skin, had never been where there were no people. Was Bimini a deserted island? One road led past shanties, a dock, and the

Bacardi Hotel at its south end. He beamed with pride at catching a large grouper which he filleted for dinner aboard the Choy Lee. Both Herb and Chris marveled at the delicate, delicious wine and butter preparation done on an alcohol stove. Served over grits with minced vegetables, the fish was a gourmet delight, and, as Alvin admitted, came as an invention with ingredients aboard.

After dinner, they talked of old movies. Did you see *Cool Hand Luke* with Paul Newman? How about *One Potato, Two Potato* with Beth Barry, Alvin asked? Or *Noting but a Man?* Chris's favorite was *Lion in Winter* with O'Tool and Hepburn. And *One Flew Over the Coo Coo's Nest* with Nicholson. Herb liked *Pink Panther* flicks and hemorrhaged with laughter at *The Russians Are Coming*–the best line was Muriel the post mistress who discovers her old man in the kitchen gagged, tied to a chair, struggling, and hanging on a coat hook, and says, "Walter, what are you doing on the wall? But *Rapture* with Dean Stockwell blew him away—the best foreign film ever. Did he think *Blowup* was over-rated? Chris asked. What about *Camelot*? Too Hollywood. "Come on," Herb replied, "Burton whacked Redgrave a major elbow to the nose in a love scene and they left it in."

He intended to teach Alvin and Chris how to play pinochle, but the discussion ended with cocktails and songs. Unexpectedly, Chris displayed a rich contralto range, mellow and soothing, and a delight to hear with lyre accompaniment as she sang *Beth Allen* and a medieval sestina, *You Goat-Herd Gods*, and then a *Dansa* in troubadour style. Hers was Alvin's first lyre experience. He drummed on two upside-down pots and did *The Four Walls Blues.* There was a future in the cool shifts and rhythmic tenor of his rendition. Herb's *Row, Row, Row Your Boat* got over-sung with a great followup of *Anything You Can Do, I Can Do Better.* The evening wound down with a commentary on astronomy as the trio sat in the cockpit beneath the stars.

"The universe hoards love and eternity," Herb said. "But catch a falling star, and you'll have them. Look, there's one," he pointed.

"How far to eternity?" Alvin asked.

"The answer rests in a Van Cliburn performance of *Tchaikovsky's Piano Concerto Number One* at the Nixon White House," Chris said.

"Were you there, Miss Chris?" he asked.

"On beautiful nights like this, I still am," she replied.

The trio packed some comforts and took the dinghy ashore. The decision to sleep that night on warm sand instead of on the yacht was a bad one.

Might any of them think that if they were asleep on the boat, the intruders would not have gotten out of hand anyway? At some point in the middle of the night, Herb awoke. In sleep, people often sense danger as if premonitions emanate from the subconscious. An alarm as surely as if we'd set one for a pre-appointed wake-up time brings us to wakefulness. Herb sat up abruptly. A half-moon shed visibility a distance in all directions. Was it the scuffling of an animal in the brush or the lapping of waves on the sand that woke him? The stars watched silently as he scanned for movement, and that's when he heard a hollow arrhythmic whomp, thud, whomp like soft mallets on tympani heads. A skiff tied off beside the Choy Lee gently played her hull. Unlocked, she lay open to scavengers from the sea. The bright moon lit a phantom moving about the cockpit. Herb nudged Alvin. The boy started up as if a bad dream were now reality. His eyes went directly to the prowler ducking into the sloop's cabin. They decided that a shore invasion came next on the agenda. So Chris was also gently awakened. She understood as soon as she saw a dinghy whopping the Choy Lee. They folded blankets, took all belongings, and went for a hideaway among trees and underbrush.

Watching the violated sloop from a shrub enclosed den, Herb thought through what was still aboard. It was a vexing inventory though some personal stuff came ashore and lay wrapped in blankets. Navigation equipment, radio, clothes, Chris's purse and jewelry, Herb's watch—a pass-me-down from his dad—and gold rope chain were among other items now changing ownership. What if the scofflaw decided to sink the sloop as an apt punishment for the absence of cash? Or worse, what if the renegade took the boat for drug running? Herb whispered to Alvin, "Stay with Chris." He decided to launch a surprise attack on the intruder. He asked for a switchblade, if Alvin had one. But the request was broken off mid-sentence.

Herb's head jerked back as a fist bunched his hair and pulled. The flat of a machete caught him under the chin. Its razor sharp blade hurt his Adam's apple. He heard a gruff, "No trash or you be dead, mon." The first flash was for friends. "Run," he commanded. Alvin grabbed Chris and made for the road down the center of Bimini. Hopefully he remembered civilization lay a distance to the south. Safety lay with Bimini's dock master or hotel personnel. Nothing to the north promised refuge. It was a desolate dead end where well-being might easily be lost to these rats, one who held a knife and the other aboard the sloop.

The Bahamian seemed pissed at the unexpected outburst, *run*. The blade of his machete met flesh, and Herb felt it sting his neck. Instinctively he went for the machete. A push back caused the attacker to loose his balance. He stumbled over a decayed log and took Herb down with him. The two sat, Herb on a boney lap. If a throat pondered its own slitting, it would demand a counter stand. And Herb did as his neck implored by whamming the crook of a knife wielding arm. He flattened it out along with the torso attached to it. They lay in a clump of sand burrs and grass. The Bahamian winced from the stickers in his bare back. Herb's shirt caught some instead of his flesh. The two men jumped up. Not realizing the blood stains were his, he felt strong and confident. They struggled for the machete. Palm fronds of a saw palmetto scratched Herb's arm. His back slammed into a tree trunk. Fumbling in the underbrush, each man vied to dominate. In a test of size, Herb lost. With new-found fitness, he held his own. A chain-gang brawn came from his adversary. Arms around Herb's middle, the Bahamian lifted a prof's full weight off the ground. Grunts, gnashing of teeth, groans, twisting, thrashing. And a body whip threw Herb off balance. The hulky arm reached for its machete. Herb kicked it away. Then the guy went for another body hug. Herb broke free by twisting. He found testicles to knee and a wrist to bite which relinquished the blade. Thank God for a seaman's balance. Herb gained footing over his adversary and wielded the purloined machete before the ape recovered from being doubled over in pain.

The guy raised both arms to protect his face. "Oh please, mon, don't make this sorry child a kilt one," he lilted in a now charming island cadence.

"Fuck you," Herb said. The beefy hellion looked to be no more than an overgrown teen. "Call your daddy off my boat. Now." The sharp machete poked at the kid's sternum.

"Look, mon, you bloody all over. Me do that to American friend?"

"Fuck you," Herb said as Alvin leapt over a dune from the road. His switchblade glistened in the moonlight.

"Miss Chris be safe," he said. "She going for help at the hotel."

The Bahamian plucked stickers from his arms and as far around back as he could reach. Little winces were audible.

"Call your partner off my boat. I"m not telling you again, shit head."

"God be my witness, you bleeding bad, Mr. Herb." Alvin whipped off his shirt and wrapped it around Herb's neck.

"Thanks, Alvin. I never realized—"

"I'll take hold the machete if you need tend to yourself."

"I'm okay."

Kerry, a name the captain and his galley mate would soon learn, pleaded for a safe surrender. He began pulling sand burrs from his pants. Herb almost laughed at the shivering novice who took orders like a slave about to be beaten. Kerry's cohort aboard the Choy Lee called for mercy from the boss man menacing a poor child ashore. Perhaps both thieves believed that on a desolate beach vengeance needn't fear law enforcement if any existed after midnight on so small an island. Human screams sounded like dolphin cries to islanders a distance away. And the Gulfstream carried dead men far from the scene of a crime. Both thieves seemed truly spooked.

As the shore crew waited for a shadow to row up on the beach, Alvin tied strips of a towel around Herb's neck in case a jaunt for the law started any bleeding again. He pulled sand burrs from Herb's shirt. Although not totally sure, he told Herb the cut was more a scratch than anything. Other strips they used to bind hellion hands behind backs. When sidekick Jarvis came to shore, Herb took the thief's Bowie knife. In a cooler stolen from the Choy Lee, there sat numerous food stuffs gathered from their on-board storage holds. He had the man leave the cooler on the beach, turn his skiff over and stomp on it until a foot went though the hull. Then the foursome started down the road toward the hotel. Jarvis gimped along because one leg used tiptoes to match the other. His silvery, kinky hair receded like the half-moon, and his broad shoulders swung into the lead of his short leg. Except for a distended beer belly, he seemed quite fit for a man old enough to be his partner's father. He said nothing as if the conquering tribe were about to decapitate the invading one. It was Kerry who started the plea. "Me pap and me, mon, came away without no pinch from your sailboat. Now you think it best to let us man free?"

"Not tonight, pal," Herb said.

"What you be after, taking us down the road, mon?"

"Life in prison, I hope," Herb said.

"Now the stealing me put the boy up to sure ain't his doing," Jarvis said. "Good God fearing Christian men might let him go home to mum where him going before him met me."

"Jarvis your pa?" Alvin asked.

"Who wants to know," the boy said.

"Me, myself, and I," Alvin said. "You got a look tells me you be family."

114

Checking both captors, Kerry observed, "You having a look to tell me you ain't brothers, mon."

"Don't be sassy mouth Kerry me boy. These be good men, lawful men me tried to hurt."

Surely Kerry could have run off into the darkness as easily as a rabbit avoids a predator, but Jarvis would have a tough time outrunning anyone. Their companionship seemed bonded in home life not criminality. And what drove a father to teach his son to pillage? On an island with such sparse population was it merely coincidence father and son happened upon a likely treasure trove? Were they scavenging for food? Perhaps the answer lay in their old, heel worn, back-broken shoes, the threadbare, hole dotted safari shorts, or the olive, Sears workman shirt minus some buttons Jarvis had knotted above his gut. Except for an accidently cut throat, what harm had these docile Bahamians wreaked? Was it principle that drove the foursome on toward the Bacardi Hotel to seek justice? Was it guilt that drove the downcast Bahamians passively onward toward humiliation and imprisonment?

"Me sorry, mon," Kerry said. "At me hut down a piece me mum can nurse a cut neck."

"The authorities will settle this," Herb said.

For men about to face law enforcement, these guilty parties seemed overly fatalistic or optimistically carefree. Perhaps Bahamian law wasn't terribly harsh with thieves, or maybe a crime committed off shore wasn't within jurisdiction? How absurd. This case was clear cut with victims and perpetrators, proof of harm, purloined goods sitting on the beach, and a citizen's arrest. If there were a trial, the two crooks would luck out as Herb had no intension of returning to Bimini or any other island to prosecute. Tonight's lesson and a brief incarceration needed to suffice. Although his neck stung, it stopped bleeding and the first aid kit on the Choy Lee had astringents and anti-infection medications so that this vacation would go on uninterrupted. He knew Alvin and Chris well enough to know they wouldn't be spooked or hesitant to continue on unless they felt Herb needed a doctor which seemed nonsensical at this point and in this place.

The dirt and gravel of a moonlit King's Highway became brighter as the men approached a lone floodlight of the hotel and a lamppost by a gas pump on the dock behind it. Somewhere a generator hummed. The Bacardi's lawn had mostly crabgrass among bald coral heads and every window in the three story structure was dark, the only inside light shown through windows of the lobby onto the front patio. Clouds over the Bimini lagoon lay like rumpled laundry beside the silvery moon. The caw, caw, caw of wildlife in wilderness surrounding the inlet wasn't identifiable. A tinge of seaweed-rot seasoned the momentarily still air. The concrete steps to the patio had no railing . Chris met them at the door as the foursome entered.

A Brit in charge also served as head of customs and, rather than take custody of Jarvis and Kerry, began an identification interrogation of Herb and Alvin as if Bimini were about to arrest criminal trespassers. Much like bureaucrats wielding power in America, this agent couldn't hear of the attack perpetrated on the beach. It became difficult to cover the anger between Herb and an officer with his hand on a pistol belted to his waist who demanded immediate unfettering of Jarvis and Kerry. Chris's objections met with obstinance, and since the officer seemed about to draw his weapon, Herb untied the captives. Interestingly enough, they did not run nor attempt to leave, but stood crestfallen as if to receive the punishment deserved. Yet, on the Brit went about the illegality of entering a country without proper identification. He would have none of the explanation that the trio's driver's licenses, credit cards, vehicle registrations and such were either aboard the boat or hidden in a cubbyhole on the beach. When the custom's agent drew his gun, Herb had visions of Kent State and became nervous. He calmly asked Chris and Alvin to comply with the man's wishes.

"Jarvis," said the agent, "there's flour, some lard, and a jar of currant jelly in the kitchen. Take the bloody provisions home to the missus. I do not take kindly to pilfering stories about either of you. Go."

"Thank you, Mr. Laughton, sir. Yes sir," Jarvis said, and he and the boy walked through a dining room off the lobby.

"Now. This matter of identity will hold until tomorrow. I am bloody tired and sorry to lock you all up for the night, but Dennis Laughton has never been accused of dereliction of duty." With that final ultimatum, the agent drew his gun and marched the trio across the one road to a two story customs house and into a holding cell barely large enough for one prisoner let alone three. Herb, Alvin, and Chris sat scrunched knee to knee on a concrete floor and played twenty questions, I-spy-with-my-little-eye, and story-building while the sun slept and they didn't.

Chapter Twenty

Mid morning, a beige-uniformed man wearing a visor-brimmed hat with a royal crown insignia brought Herb's wallet, Chris's canvas purse, Alvin's student identification within a polyester back pack and all their beached possessions—blankets tied together, snorkeling paraphernalia, air-pillows and mattresses, marshmallows and crunchy snacks, boxed matches, Coleman lantern—to the tight holding cell. Opening it, he led them from the custom house porch, down its stark white steps, through the sunshine of a crude, tropical wonderland, across the gravely King's Highway, back to the three story Bacardi Hotel, and into a dining room where they sat at a white-clothed, round table with five place settings. Much to their amazement, a white jacketed waiter brought a bowl of fresh fruit—bananas, oranges, and mamey—along with a basket of fresh, hot rolls and butter, iced water, and a carafe of aromatic coffee. The cold water disappeared before anything else. Herb wanted to shower, brush his teeth, shave, and change clothes, but decided that a quiet cup of coffee wouldn't press any issues with the local authorities. Without fanfare or explanation, the officer joined them at the table. Other than *pass the butter* and *this, whatever, oh, mamey, it's delicious* the hungry crew ate. When eggs, bacon, and sausage came family style, the officer apologized for the inconvenience of last night's accommodations. He asked forgiveness for Dennis Laughton's unfortunate actions, but rum-runners and smugglers sailed these waters. Would the Americans accept breakfast gratis from the Bahamian Government? And a night at the Bacardi came with the meal. The Choy Lee, now docked outside, was unmolested for the next leg of the journey. The next morning when Herb settled the emergency berth tab, restocking, and towing charges with the dock master, he thoroughly understood the hollow *gratis* of the Bahamian Government. Accepting the check-in offer for a room at the Bacardi, the threesome, after washing, hit the beds like cell mates at lights out and slept the afternoon away in a room with twin beds and a Castro Convertible sofa.

The conch salad and Bahamian Lobster at dinner gave the trio, now refreshed and groomed, cuisine to rave about. Everything tasted fresh, nicely seasoned, newly prepared, and masterfully garnished. Yet proper service seemed unfamiliar to the waiter. Not one course came out timely. The stuffed potatoes waited for desert time, while key lime pie sat at the table from mid-meal. Conch chowder and entrees came simultaneously or backwards. Nonetheless, Herb tipped as if he were in the States. Using a phone in the lobby to try to reach his mom, Herb couldn't get a long distance operator or a dial tone to Ma Bell although advised by the desk clerk to wait until the Bahamian phone company took positive action for its foreign customer. He ended up calling Miami on the ship to shore radio aboard the Choy Lee.

Near sunset, a visit to Bimini's only general store opened the visitors' eyes. Other than a half-dozen or so canned string beans, corn, and lima beans, sparse tackle, and rancid bait, the mostly empty wood-slat shelves contained nothing purchasable by American standards in a store half the size of a one car garage. A rusty coca cola cooler contained Styrofoam buoys for mooring lines or lobster pots. Down the road, several huts lay nestled in the tropical brush lining the King's Highway, Bimini's gravel road that ran seven miles end to end. Mildewed white or faded, ocean blue paint dominated all but the pink customs house and the deep green Bacardi Hotel. Rowboats, lobster traps, bicycle parts, motor props, engine parts, broken masts, booms, hatch covers, rods and reels, and other salvaged stuff lay against the occasional concrete blocked, thin stuccoed, one or two room dwellings with makeshift roofs of galvanized metal, tar paper, composition roll, or gravel. The overgrown yards seemed machete-cleared for access to homes which weren't much larger than guardhouses in American communities. Walking by, it was possible to see paths through mangroves behind these places that led to small, makeshift docks or lagoon shallows where a native might launch his skiff.

Bare feet, a few bicycles, and an occasional Vespa Honda traveled the mostly empty road of North Bimini which suggested water craft as native and visitor preferred transportation. Few people in sight also indicated that the island's population rivaled that of Stovepipe Wells in Death Valley. Un-desert like, the island's weather felt moderate and a tropical breeze animated its native canopy of greenery—eastern shoreline mangroves; clusters of gumbo limbos, some with strangler figs; medicinal lignum vitaes; high casuarinas; clumps of seagrapes; cocoplums, and an occasional coconut palm.

Before moon-rise, the stars needed eye-tending because of their bright prominence. An occasional candle flicker or kerosene lamp from huts where natives perhaps told adventure stories before bedtime diverted young, touristy eyes from the heavens. By early evening at the hotel, a bartender and one waitress served a barroom with probably as many guests as natives. As Herb, Chris, and Alvin entered, local musicians began to play bongos, steel drums, banjo, and concertina. The lead singer had placed a hand written sign against the podium which read *Ronnie and the Ramblers*. In a lilting Bahamian style, the man sang about a native woman, *brown as coconut, soft as summer breeze, she cheat at poker and at love.* Herb and Chris were new to the upbeat, island sound which Alvin told them was Goombay music. These were story songs, one following the other, with codas of barber shop harmony, as Chris described them. "Berma Road," "Bahama Rock," and "Crow Calypso" followed one another non-stopped as Bacardi Rum, dark or light, with a mix of one's choice, coke, seven up, or lime and soda, being the only selections other than house wine served up from a handwritten menu. And this evening, the establishment was out of ice so along with the weather, the drinks were tepid.

Of particular interest to Herb was a gimpy, older man who swept the cantilevered dock adjacent to the open air bar. The sighting brought his palm up to a bandaged cut on his neck sterilized earlier with stinging alcohol and first aid cream. With a rum and coke in hand, he walked out to the familiar janitor, sat at one of the tables, and waited for the native to notice. It took Jarvis only a few moments before he bowed and backed away. Herb followed him into a storage room beside the dock where, upon entering, he saw the man hanging the broom and dust pan. "We spent a night in jail instead of you and Kerry," Herb announced pointedly.

"Me a deeply sorry man for carrying a stranger food in me only work-boat," Jarvis said without turning to face a dissatisfied customer.

"You might work for a living or beg instead of stealing. What if your son accidently killed a person?"

"Him a good boy, mon."

"A boy who needs a good father."

Jarvis turned abruptly. With squinted eyes, he fired a stare at Herb that flashed defiance. "Me try hard to work, mon."

Undaunted, unmoved, unsympathetic, Herb shot back, "Not hard enough."

Jarvis went for the door as though self-justifications were useless and replied dismissively, "Bosses not passing round good work no more on Bimini Islands."

Herb leaned against the door. "What about this janitor job?"

"Pay for things Mr. Laughton sold us last night." Jarvis picked up a mop handle as if he meant to retrieve his Bowie knife from Herb. "Bimini folk live off the water and the rich tourist like you, mon. Me do the nets, slings, scuba stuff, engine repair, and work up the nasty parts to run again, Mr. Rizer, mon."

"You know my name?"

"Bimini Island a small place. You in me way, mon."

Herb remained against the door. "Why teach your kid to steal?"

Jarvis reached for a mop head and clipped it on its handle. "American man think him know about life in the island." He placed it in the mop bucket, plunged, set it in the

121

vee, and pulled the press. "For all a pretty boat, nice clothes, good fresh food, free time and dollar you waste, who you steal from when the man back is turned?"

"Whoa. I work hard. When times are bad, I make do."

"Me think you man not seeing bad times."

"What does that mean?"

Jarvis hesitated, rolled the mop and bucket aside, and slumped down on a stack of pool chemicals in plastic buckets. He seemed a prisoner at rest before sentencing. "A grandchild come for me woman to feed when she mama die. And me junk don't find the dollar yesterday, today, and yet again tomorrow. That trouble for rich man America?" He rolled the mop and bucket toward Herb. "Out me way. Me work to be doing."

Herb opened the door. "You ever scrape the bottom of a sailboat?"

"Sure as a barnacle stick to him home. Think this bad foot can drown a man?"

"What do you charge?"

"What do a rich man pay? Ten, fifteen dollar?"

"More if my boat's finished by early morning?"

"How bad the bottom?"

"I don't know. Here's five. You'll get you're pay if the job's done."

And a few hours after sunup, the bottom of the Choy Lee claimed to be barnacle free. Kerry and Jarvis, slick as chocolate in a double boiler, spread a few handfuls of crushed shells on the dock as proof. Four twenties, a ten, and a five dollar bill passed clandestinely into Jarvis's palm. Gratefully, it wasn't counted in front of Alvin or Chris who surely became bollixed up when two snorkelers, former assailants, surfaced from under the Choy Lee. Was cash a curative or a curse for the impoverished? Would Jarvis and family use the overpayment wisely or would the next boat anchoring off shore in Bimini become another unsuspecting treasure trove? As the trio sailed east, the lyrics of Brecht's beggar's reprieve replayed in Herb's head: *What keeps a man alive?/He lives on others/He likes to taste them first/then eat them whole if he can/Forgets that they're supposed to be his brothers/ that he himself was ever called a man/Remember if you wish to stay alive/For once do something bad/and you'll survive.*

Chapter Twenty-One

Before sailing the Bahama Bank, Jarvis had advised to look out for coral heads. "A bloke on the bow lookout, mon," he'd said. Alvin got a little spooked listening to the Bahamian. "Coral heads be easy to spot in sunlight and clear water," Jarvis went on. At low tide, some poked the surface and made waves. Big boats, Herb listened to the experienced Bahamian, were better off rounding the island and sailing into the Tongue of the Ocean. "Tides be devils here and safe water turn on you fast as a false-hearted woman," he said tossing the dock lines aboard the Choy Lee as Herb revved her engine. About anchoring in coral—"You'll be bloody, mon, diving to get twisty flukes while friends be wearing life gear and praying Jesus they not next on the rocks." Herb'd learn later that channel markers were after thoughts and the chart for the Bahamas was a toddler compared to the US Coast and Geodetic Survey ones. Perhaps the shallows were correct on the Bahamian navigation tool, but no coral heads appeared anywhere on it. Nonetheless, the original plan called for crossing the bank and that's what Herb did. Going around the Bahama Bank meant missing Chub Cay as well as several days and nights of non-stopped sailing.

Jarvis and Kerry waved as the Choy Lee motored out of the Bimini marina toward a watery horizon. Somewhere lay Chub Cay with its clubhouse and golf course. A sandy bottom glided under the sloop on an almost cloudless azure day with favorable breezes. She heeled gently into ripples of windswept water. Sloshes from the bone in her teeth sounded like a rushing brook. Reflections on the freeboard were like a school of guppies ever swirling. In morning sunshine, a shadow from the sails and mast skipped along the leeward side close to the sloop's water line. Alvin then Chris stood watch on the bow whenever Herb saw changes in the underwater hues.

He dead reckoned the position of a lone spar at the heart of the Bahama Bank on a leg toward protected harbor.

Alvin marveled at the ability to find a stick in the middle of the ocean without road signs, arrows, railroad tracks or sidewalks to follow, without asking directions, or trailing someone. He undoubtedly had doubts about the whereabouts of Bimini until Herb explained the workings of a radio direction finder. But Chris also congratulated the captain on his marksmanship. Missing this marker meant sailing into the Tongue of the Ocean, earth's deepest water, and traveling all night to Nassau which excluded a stop at the club for dinner and rest. The Bahama Bank was unforgiving to vessels in night travel.

They dropped anchor near a triangle-topped spar adorned with an anhinga. Its gray and black wings unfolded like a kite ready for flight without anyone to run the string. The Choy Lee feathered into the wind nicely as the crew furled the sails and tied them off. The ceremonial sun neared its twilight chambers on a carpet of low clouds. The whitecaps became stark as they scurried across darkening water. By the end of battening the sloop down for the night, twilight doffed a veil over a watery mirror. Jarvis hadn't mentioned the rough go of anchoring in unprotected water. The Choy Lee rolled and bucked so that the chef couldn't stabilize a pot on the stove. A chili dinner became baloney and cheese sandwiches and soda. Herb wanted the landlubber chef to take Dramamine thereby avoiding sea sickness, but Alvin refused. Chris didn't decline, and shortly after dinner, conked out on the settee.

Alvin needed outside air. Becoming woozy himself, Herb joined him. Fresh, stiff breezes settled stomachs. Sitting in the cockpit under backlit clouds illuminated by a bold moon and a dome of uncountable stars, Alvin put his arm around his friend. "Mr. Captain Man, we all happy, and we ain't drowned." The clanging of main and jib sheets on an aluminum mast sounded like wind chimes. Other than a random, low hum of breezes finding hollows through a hatch or portal, the night chorus let the vast ocean silence fill its loft. Alvine went on, "Rufus got no idea the changes you put this here boy through." He massaged Herb's scruff. "One day there be a book about old Herb, and I know a brother like to write about him."

Herb leaned against a cushion, clasped his palms behind his head, and put his feet up on the captain's chair. "In your story, does he find a girl who loves him?"

Alvin slid a smidgen away and placed his palms on his knees. But for harmonizing himself with the rocking of the boat, he seemed tense. When he spoke, it came in a near whisper. "She be waiting one scoot away."

Herb blanched at the honesty. Alvin looked down on the teak below his bare feet. Would a teacher, an almost brother, a friend, cross over? He cupped a palm over his crotch, scissored his thighs, and shot a look. Herb smiled. Suddenly, a cry came from the choppy water. A school of dolphins broke the surface. The creatures almost brushed the hull of the Choy Lee, their oversized playmate. Their clicks and calls sounded like toddlers in daycare. As they circled and passed, Herb noticed the mammals were so close they almost brushed one another, so close one breaking torso raised several tails above the surf, so close dorsal fins cut the water in unison. Was love closer than this, a dance done with frivolity? When the show ended, he glanced at Alvin sitting with legs together, hands folded, and eyes downcast waiting, waiting, *One scoot away.* "Have you ever been with a girl, Alvin?"

"Used to tell myself try it. But pap made me different early on."

"Oh, God. Are you telling me—"

"Listen up. Pap doing his thing in Moultrie at Lee and Rem's without no son to beat on. What's done is done and gone." Alvin fisted his palm and his thighs clamped together. "Alvin asking, do Mr. Herb try the other way?"

Herb gazed up at the stars as if a reprieve lay somewhere in the heavens. "I'm caught on a wild merry-go-round that won't quit."

"They's other amusement parks in this here world. Alvin can show you one has rides wild as any you ever been on."

"Is Alvin in love with Rufus?" Herb asked.

His thighs began their game again as he pulled off his shirt for the night breeze to cool his taught body. "Not like you and Miss Beth, if that's what you be thinking. Rufus mostly need someone to boss. Alright for a time, but he don't know what love is."

"Do you?"

"Start with desire, move on to deep respect, come into worship, worry, heartsickness, hebegeebees, and waiting at a locked gate you want a certain bro to open, let you in, because he want you."

"Beth locked that gate, and though I think of a thousand reasons why, I can't accept any of them."

"Alvin know the feeling."

"She rules my thoughts, Alvin. You, better than anyone, understand. If I had no one to listen to my craziness, I'd crack. I'm not sure my pieces are together anyway."

Alvin folded his shirt neatly onto the seat. "You ain't hot?" he asked.

Herb shook his head. Desire seemed unmanageable these days. His physical and spiritual selves had become entwined when Beth first said—*do you believe minds can superimpose, two hearts become one. Yes*, he'd said in reruns. *Yes, I believe,* he'd repeated in dreams. That first night in her bed ended a man once surefooted, purposeful, goal oriented, peaceful, and self-reliant. She caused him to flee his apartment, to be addicted to work, to bear sexual displacement. He heard himself say aloud, "How do you stop loving?" as if Alvin had mastered emotional overflow with a secret, shutoff valve.

A deep-rooted honesty came from the boy. "Alvin imagine boys, nope, he mean men, desire forbidden fruit. They wants what can't be had. Crazy urges be hard to jail up. You follow, Mr. Herb? I think love be what you can't reach, not what you can." For the first time, Alvin's deep, brown eyes fixed on Herb without any glance away as if his convictions were as solid as the Choy Lee. He unreservedly went on, "Rufus the first to crow around my coop. He protect me any which way he can. We good for each other from the get go."

Herb pondered Beth in her second-time-around marriage. Did she want *what couldn't be reached,* Samuel Shockett, a husband who handed her over to a delivery room hypnotist and horrid agony in child bearing was, he thought, why she suffered unfinished business. But Herb had rejuvenated her, doted on her, worshiped her. How was it now possible that she rejected the beauty of their affair? How was it possible to negate what happened up to Key West? "A few guys like Dr. Shockett are lucky as shit," Herb offered sheepishly.

"Alvin's champeen can't see bad dirt he toss onto good."

"I don't understand."

"Alvin worship the man who buried a pa's ashes in dark night in a angry cemetery that told him to fuck off. Buried his pa 'cause it was right. Being there, Alvin'd buried his own hurt just like Herb done at that grave. Alvin pray a thousand times for a right smart teacher who want to hump a double-crossing Delilah, a girl who put the law on him."

The pause in conversation let the chimes, flaps, and rigging whistles of a sloop at rest in Bahama breezes entertain the deep, lonesome night. "Ever think about having children of your own?" Herb asked.

"God fixes some men for other ways."

The response came packaged honestly but not considerately. "Maybe your dad *fixed* you prematurely. Women are splendid creatures worthy of love."

Irritation rode the edges of Alvin's words. "Let Alvin take you into a man bar and see us dance. Then say muscle and might makes no never mind."

"Sorry if I insulted you, buddy."

"Just open the gate, brother."

"Not now."

Herb went below and poured cups of rum and coke. Outside, they sipped until the choppy water curbed along with the strong pitch of the Choy Lee. On and off dozing on a rocking boat wasn't easy, and by sunrise, the trio was more than ready to set sail. Once underway, the sloop heeled over and glided along like a child on a water slide. Alvin cooked a hot breakfast of bacon and cheese omelets with Texas toast and brewed great coffee. By afternoon they were anchored off shore at Chub Cay's magnificent white, sandy beach where they swam and loafed until sunset. It wasn't until after dinner that Herb told about an encounter with a shark which was why he came through the shallows for them with a dinghy.

Snorkeling toward the boat from the beach, Herb saw a large fish bottom feeding between him and the sloop. The brown giant glided across sea grass and halved an amber jack, head still gasping for air and the rest swallowed as a quick lunch. The dorsal fin caught Herb's eye as the animal rolled. Its nose lifted from the grassy bottom where it devoured the thrashing head of its prey. Herb swam like hell for the beach. His heart pounded fiercely. The shark must have sensed it—thud, thud, thud in his chest, his head, his ears. The animal'd be at his scissoring legs in a moment. He fought panic. Would he forfeit toes, a foot, what? His life? His mind whirled. Why hadn't he carried a knife? The snorkel seemed an only weapon. That, and a fist which in water moved so slowly as to be devoured by razor teeth itself. He turned to face the thing. The shark, too, suspended itself above the grass swishing its nose in sand as if sharpening for an attack. He waited head on so that the animal might see the full measure of its prey. The snorkel came from his mouth. He lay ready to kick, flail, punch, pound—whatever was needed to sustain life, to come out of the battle as whole as possible. Then, as if Herb didn't exist, the shark turned and meandered away. The trio joked and laughed over the story, but agreed from then on they'd all carry knives.

Herb got to shower last in a head which opened directly to the forward state room where he crawled under sheets. An open hatch scooped a comfortable breeze through the boat, and lying on his back with hands cupped behind his head, he tried to identify star patterns. Between the bunks on the teak floor, moonlight made a square of shiny teak which shifted as the boat calmly oscillated on the anchor line. A shooting star streaked across the sky and fireworks fell from its tail. Sleep didn't come so he decided to read. After the trial and weak concluding chapters of Richard Wright's *Native Son, Black Like Me* came from his duffle. Before midway, he marked his place and clicked off the cabin light. Chris called goodnight from the main cabin. He wondered how long she'd been awake. Alvin wished good dreams from the aft cabin.

And the night rocked him to sleep. Bizarre, he saw Lola May Ferringer doing a Can Can at a sleazy bar in the Bowery. He and Alvin and Chris waited for the night's featured blues singer. He with a Southern Comfort Manhattan, Chris with a Jack Rose, and Alvin with a Bud in hand watched an old woman half-kick with music from a rinky-tink, gay nineties band. A raunchy *Gypsy* tune began. He recognized the *Tits and Ass* theme as Lola May did a striptease down to nipple twirlers. He waited for the inevitable heart attack. She dropped her ankle length granny skirt, twirled her blouse and tossed it. Landing at his table, it smelled acidy and old ladyish. Her breasts gyrated and fleshy arms giggled with the twirl of pom poms. As she kicked, her freckled white skin changed to deeper and deeper shades of mottled brown. When she bowed, he saw a dorsal fin. Along with the rinky-tink music, he heard gurgling like a waterfall. The barroom gushed with seawater, the dancer grew fins and a tail, and her overstretched, cartoonish smile showed rows of shiny, sharp teeth. The water encircled his ankles, waist, then chest. Submerged, he faced the wide jaws of Lola May Ferringer swimming toward him. The razor sharp teeth sat in rows behind thin lips. Wrenching loose a chair leg to defend himself, he awoke.

Not the gentle slosh of water against the hull nor the silence lulled him back to dreamland. He slipped on shorts and stood in the open doorway to the main cabin. He wasn't sure if "Chris" was said aloud or conveyed telepathically, but she raised her head and whispered his name. He took her by the hand into his forward stateroom. If he wanted gratification, he'd have felt guilt. But the breeze which gently lifted her hair, purified their togetherness. Across a shaft of moonlight, they gazed at each other. When she reached for him, he took her hand and kissed it. He turned on the light, and she winced. "Thanks for everything," he said. She nodded, took his hand, and held it to her cheek before reaching to turn the light off and pulling him beside her on the bed. She smelled sweet and briny. They hugged for a while before she whispered, "I want you to want me." Her bikini panties and tee-shirt felt warm against him.

Why? seemed as un-lame a reply as any that came to mind for a valued friend he wished to keep.

"Because I"m thirty," she whispered. "Because I validate your social facade."

"I love you as a friend."

She pinched his nose between her fingers. "Oh, silly boy, I want a license and a ceremony with gala reception, debutante style."

"You wouldn't be happy with me."

"I'd offer freedom to indulge in your—your— But together, we'd come home to each other always."

"It sounds nice, but you deserve better."

"I—I—"

"I'd change your situation if the power was within me. Please don't cry."

"I don't want to. But—but—God damn it—don't go ape-shit with me. It's so stupid, but I do love you. Ours is a nice story together. For you, I'd dump the orange furniture and Romantic fakes on my walls. I'd become a Jewess in training. I'd quit teaching and become a mother if you asked. I think you've know since that first night at Sir John's. You must realize by now that this gratification I've foisted on you, is selfish on my part. I love you. Does that make me less of a friend?"

He turned with this back to her. "Oh God."

She petted his shoulder. "I'm sorry, but I do. We don't

have to ever fuck."

He grinned wryly.

"One day, you'd love me. And life together would become whole. Why brush me off?"

He faced her. "God! It's me. It's me. Not you. I'm so hung up on being shafted, on faithlessness, on fear of loving or being loved. I'm so fucked up it's pathetic."

"Please don't cry. Please. I love you."

Her finger wiped tears away. She kissed him again and again. Truth rose in his shorts like the renegade Peter to make his protest known. Was there no end to deceit, to wanton arousal? Motherly kisses became French tonguing as hands foraged for sustenance. They removed garments accustomed to guarding friendship. Crying had wet a sluice for the onrush of emotion. The frenzy in the stateroom went well beyond doubts of a pragmatic, aging woman and the celibacy of a betrayed lover. If Chris rode the crest of vanity because a gay guy aroused her womanhood, Herb rode the divergent paths of body over spirit. She huffed erotically. She panted rhythmically. Neither anticipated the unbridled coupling in the moonlit stateroom. Both sweated with passions un-cooled by tropical breezes.

Their coming climaxes would have changed friendship had they not been frightened by a tap on the stateroom door which opened without hesitation. In freeze frame, Herb glanced at the doorway. In the semi-dark frame, a body posed. Its stillness freaked at the now paused goings on but did not rush from the scene. Herb's eyes followed the caramel figure to the foot of the wide settee where it sat statue-like awaiting a rebuff. When none came, Alvin scooted under the sheet and entwined himself in the tryst.

Herb felt a new layer of warm flesh. Two heads hovered, and their lips met, held, melded, purred gently like a kitten grooming itself. Chris's lips went down to their former home against Herb's while Alvin's moved to the back of his neck. When Herb flinched, Chris whispered, "It's okay. He loves you." She eased Herb from her womanly portal and nudged Alvin between them. When a man's lips found Herb's, they felt as soft and loving as the worship that brought them there. A musk scent widened Herb's nostrils. A perceptible gasp of delight, of satisfaction, of hope, of anticipation stirred his eardrums. He tasted the saline of Alvin's kiss, watched the chestnut forehead rock passionately, felt a probing tongue stretch his lips. Then as Alvin turned to Chris, Herb felt himself slowly and easily guided into a region tight and warm and moist. The movement of Alvin against him and then toward Chris had strange intrigue. He wanted Chris, but she was taken. He wanted himself instead, but he was alternately served. The sound of flesh against flesh had an erotic quality as three voices cried their nearly simultaneous climaxes. Except for the hyper breathing, the frenzy slowed then ceased. What began in trio ended in trio as the captain and crew slept as one, peacefully and soundly, until daybreak.

Necessary and not so necessary chores consumed time until breakfast. In close quarters each was beset with remorse, elation, satisfaction, disquiet, hope, and confusion which invaded secret spheres of muddled intellects. When Alvin put his palm on Herb's thigh and Chris rested her head on his shoulder, he said, "We'd best sail for home." By nightfall they were in the Gulfstream and by daybreak, tying off at Coconut Grove Marina from where the Choy Lee had been rented. Alvin took off in his truck and Herb dropped Chris off at Tara. The trio had sailed together and made love together. Each was enhanced yet diminished. Only the Choy Lee remained unchanged. It awaited a next hurricane when the storm surge raised it above the dock spars, and she'd be breached, scuttled, and sunk. Alvin would live a fantasy paralyzed by fact. Herb would feel the guilt of carnality. Chris would show her pregnancy late in the term and tell her mother a few weeks before labor set in. The male child she'd bare at a hospital in Plymouth looked like a red-skinned Harry Belafonte.

Chapter Twenty-Two

After Chub Cay, Chris began dating Pastor Roeby Williamson of the First Baptist Church in Miami. That he was several years her senior did not bother the Currys. That he wasn't a Methodist seemed tolerable. That he was Mensa pleased the doctor immensely. That she did not inform Herb led to complications. After an evening at Friar Tucks to hear Dixieland done Rollo style, Herb took her to Tyler's afterward. She seemed distant and unmoved by music which usually stirred her evaluative nature. He'd pretty much decided after Chub Cay that bringing Alvin along as an appendage on their engagements had been unfair. Had he delved into personal motives certainly friendship dominated, but after Chub Cay any safety net for pseudo, insidious promises and commitments came down. Chris deserved the truth as well as his personal attention, and if his heart found hers, so be it, if not, at least honest escorting would be refreshing for both of them. Chris, on the other hand, having missed her period, began a decision making process incompatible with his agenda. As she sipped herbal tea with raisin bread and cream cheese, he broke the silence by soliciting an opinion about Rollo's dixieland.

"He's too closeted to become an honest musician," she said.

"What about his sidemen?" he asked. "Couch plays a great trombone."

"Let's not talk about jazz," she said. "Appreciating a sideman feels like yesterday for me. I'm headed for sacred music."

"Why not both?"

"They drained me."

"Can I be of service?"

"We've been down that path."

"Natalie Cole's at the Eden Roc. Are you up to it?"

"I'm begging off of soul music."

"Is the Sir John history then?"

134

"How's Alvin?"

"He's working in the dean's office now."

"You let him go?"

"I transferred him."

"You were inseparable."

"We're all understanding friends."

"Are gays that fickle?"

"I don't know."

"This is Chris talking. I've kept your secret."

"The secret is, and don't get mad, I used Alvin to keep you."

"Are you telling–"

"Sure am."

"Don't be so darn smug."

"I apologize for acting so self-serving."

"You are pathetically laughable."

"So laugh."

"This gal is done slumming around with you."

"Aren't I the safety net in a high-wire act for your dad anymore?"

"God, Herb. Were you deaf to everything I wanted?"

"I love being with you."

"Oh, you dope. You were a sexual anomaly I intended to save."

"What if you did?"

"Don't patronize me."

"Sorry I misled you."

"Oh, please. You haven't at all fooled anyone but yourself."

"Why are you so angry?"

"Take me home."

After cooling off weeks later, she invited him again to accompany the family to Dade County Auditorium for a Spring revival of *Porgy and Bess* and then to a theater season closing with *Equus* at the Coconut Grove Playhouse. After the play, she told him of Pastor Roeby Williamson whom she was to marry the following school year and of her son to be, Jonas, coming into the world. At first he thought her baiting

135

him. This woman in her fifth month looked like an actress presenting at the academy awards without showing any signs although her evening gown that night was a satin chemise. He asked about doctor's care, and since her parents were in the dark, she told him that Roeby elicited a gynecologist in his congregation. Yet it was Herb she asked to drive her to Plymouth as a partner for the delivery. He was unhesitating about two things: one; asking if the child was his, and if so, he'd marry her in a heart beat, and two; accompanying her at the hospital as Herb Curry. She laughed at his empty proposal of a union framed by mendacity and one that wouldn't work. Besides, she was certain that the baby wasn't his—of that lie, of course, she was totally unsure. Once he held the baby, he knew whose child it was. The miniature Harry Belafonte had his father's face.

Chapter Twenty-Three

Herb went again to see Alvonica McKinnon in *Porgy and Bess* at Dade County Auditorium. He invited Lorraine Shore who readily accepted her supervisor's offer. Lorraine was a meaty girl though by no means fat. She loved high hair and painstakingly teased her beehive and sprayed it religiously so that, on campus, not even a moderate breeze loosened it. Professor of Middle Eastern and Biblical Lit, she received her doctorate at Sarah Lawrence College before her twenty-second birthday and the former department head had hired her in a heartbeat. She traveled by bus from her mother's place in Shenandoah to the university because she didn't drive. When Herb became department head, he learned that a displaced Chicagoan in Greater Miami had to ride the most unreliable and worst public transportation system in the United States. It took two transfers by bus and over an hour for Lorraine to get five miles to work. Herb, being minutes away, backtracked a bit and picked her up regularly unless she had a class before eight which happened twice a week until he changed her schedule.

Standing in the lobby of Dade County Auditorium before and after *Porgy and Bess*, Lorraine had been addressed in Spanish by Salvadorans who thought her President Hernandez's ambassador to the United States. Perhaps the overdone mascara, crimson lips, and peachy-round face looked Latin, or the large, designer frames, the lenses of which enhanced her dark brown eyes, created an air of grandness. She wore a black caftan with black pearl accent jewelry that, if it weren't costume, was borrowed as her widowed mother received welfare since Lorraine's grade school years.

Herb took Lorraine back stage to meet Alvonica McKinnon who autographed their programs. The actress hugged Herb and Lorraine. She asked after his mother who hardly socialized since Sol passed on—bad for a woman alone. "Talk her into working on *A Raisin in the Sun,* The

Lycium's winter showcase. Her good friend, Aubrey Crane, is directing. Alvin's the lead. And I'll be playing his mother, of all things." Herb promised to work on Minnie. Of course Alvin, who helped with his mama's pre-performance prep and after curtain packing, came into the dressing room as Herb and his date were about to go. He and his mama were going to the Sir John Club, and why didn't Herb and Lorraine tag along? He seemed totally pissed when Herb turned down the offer. "Don't soul music be tasteful enough for your new white lady?" Alvonica castigated him for rudeness and shuffled him out. On the way back to Shenandoah, Lorraine asked why the guy seemed so unfriendly. Oh, what a story he didn't tell her. Would she have cringed at friends who crossed lines of moral propriety and distorted each other's affinities?

What Herb and Lorraine didn't do was go to any bar, booze in a clandestine pad, drag one another into nearby woods, or park on a dark street. On the way home, they talked of light situations (greeting the continually distracted English aid: "Good morning Rita." Response: "It's on the table."), Jewish geography ("Mom's from Russia." "So's mine."), losing fathers ("He suffered a massive coronary." "Minnie wouldn't allow an autopsy."), tending to mothers ("She won't go out of the house." "Mine, only when I take her to lunch."), buying a car and learning to drive ("I flunked driver's education.""I'll teach you."), and favorite movies—Herb's was *Summer and Smoke* with Lawrence Harvey—Lorraine's, *Stop the World. I Want to Get Off* with Anthony Newley.

Lorraine invited him in to meet Mrs. Shore, a gaunt, good looking, worn version of her daughter. Herb marveled at the spotless apartment kept without any professional cleaning lady. The furniture was worn and second-rate Salvation Army, like the Hollywood Bed in the combination living and dining room which Mama Shore used at night so that Lorraine had the lone bedroom to herself. Shadow boxes, a curio cabinet, and display shelves contained myriad crystal, ceramic, brass, pewter, and ivory bric-a-brac that looked antique and prized as if the family in the old country held an economic status it had lost in America. The older woman seemed pleased with Herb by the way she took his jacket, set a pillow for him on the easy chair, made coffee when it wasn't necessary, sat beside him in a folding chair, pulled over an old hassock for his feet, gave him a linen napkin when she served the coffee, and smiled profusely during her gracious but probing chat. Lorraine was mortified and apologetic. When Miss Shore walked him back to the Continental, they kissed goodnight. The evening overflowed with normality and warm, peaceful, uncomplicated feelings Herb had missed somehow in his pursuit of a soul mate.

He drove home to Dinner Key Marina and a Hunter fifty foot ketch purchased from Merrill Stevens. Heading for his slip at pier five, he found the boat open and Alvin propped on a settee in the cabin, knees tucked under his chin, and dozing. A glass with melted ice and a bottle of Southern Comfort, well tapped into, sat beside him. Herb had said nothing about giving up his place in Coral Gables, buying a boat, and moving aboard. Alvin had to be gumshoeing. A first reaction was guilt for dodging a friend, for turning continual outings together into self-imposed isolation, for transferring Alvin to the dean's office without as much as a *what do you think*, for discourteously ignoring calls on his answer machine. A no-brainer that the anger in his mama's dressing room was so pronounced.

A no-brainer that Alvin's planned confrontation tonight. Why else would he break in? Getting through the security gate at the pier and jimmying the companionway lock without attracting attention was quite a feat at Dinner Key Marina where blacks were absent. A half empty bottle indicated that the kid'd been waiting for some time. Although it might be good to talk things out, Herb wished it was on different terms and in a different place. Guilt and awkwardness hadn't totally let up. Yet Herb felt violated, pissed off, and antsy because of the break-in and spying. Sliding the companionway hatch to enter his new sloop was sufficient to startle the intruder. "How'd you get through the security gate?" Herb asked coming down the steps.

Alvin's drowsy pause gathered the indignation a forced entry intended for this now reversed ambush. His bare feet slapped down on the floor, and he un-flattened his Afro. "I got ways." He kicked back the melted ice and threw the glass which shattered at the foot of the ladder.

Herb glared at the mess on his new floorboards and fixed Alvin in his stare. "If I wanted you here, I'd've sent an invitation."

"Alvin don't give a rat's shit." He held a grab rail as if the boat were rocking instead of his head. "They's some things got to be done."

Herb stepped over the shattered glass. "Ugly *things*? Like insulting my date tonight? Like calling my answer machine?"

Alvin took a swig from the bottle then threw the Southern Comfort which smashed against the bulkhead. A peachy, alcoholic smell permeated the main cabin. "Man. Don't fuck with Alvin head."

Herb forced Alvin down on the settee. "You're drunk."

"Hope it be so, Mr. High and Mighty."

"Why are you here?"

"Take me through changes, play with my head, fuck me, but Alvin be shit. Tossed off nigger trash."

"You know that's not true. Get down to the nitty-gritty. What do you want?"

"Carry out your promises, boss man."

"And—and—promises?"

"You the one preached love-making come with soul. Then acting like one night change everything."

"I can't deal with what happened. Don't know how. Don't know why. So my head's in the sand until I do."

A knee-jerk to the groin doubled Herb in pain. Alvin lunged and clutched his neck. "Mother Fucker. I done been fucked over."

"Whoa," came out of Herb as a wimpy breath during a reverse of two bodies, one forced onto the settee and trying to groan in pain, the other, now energized, enraged, and irrational. Alvin stood over him, hands tightening, tightening, choking off the whiskey tainted, cabin air. Herb shut his eyes. If unconsciousness resulted, he'd regain it. No way was this kid going to kill his friend. Beneath the rage, love existed. And love couldn't take life. Self-reproach and guilt ran in Alvin's veins as surely as in Herb's. So trust. Herb did. Believe. He did. Wait. He did for a reprieve from the anger seditious acts of friendship spawn. There can be no unbridled anger in a kind man. There can be no murder in a sympathetic heart. There can be no ultimate vengeance in a lover. There can be no finality where finality isn't embedded.

Herb felt a coming, an arrival, an new experience, a dimming, possibly a withdrawal from lack of breath. It was like existing on the edge of hypnotic sleep. He heard heaves of raw emotion overhead, tasted his own saliva burning his tongue and rising to the sides of his mouth. Tears formed at the edges of his lids. He sensed hot, whiskey tainted breath against his forehead. Yet he did not resist. Did not struggle. The choke-hold tightened as his mind swirled toward the bottom of a whirlpool. He barely heard the anger, but would not look at it. "Cock Sucker. Play me for a fool," would have been the last, grit-teethed words if Alvin hadn't released the choke-hold and sent Herb reeling with a powerful backhand.

The mentor fell. A sharp gasp for air heightened his senses, and Herb brought a palm up to a stinging pain in his jaw. "Shit," he whispered and, looking up, saw a puffing silhouette who stood, red palms splayed, as if awaiting martyrdom. He felt warm drops of blood running across his lips and down his chin and pulled the tail of his shirt up to stop the nosebleed.

Alvin huffed like a wounded bull eyeing a matador's cape. Weeping, he said through clenched teeth, "Hit me back, Mother Fucker. Go for it. Hit me back."

"Damn it." Herb curled into a fetal position to protect his body and his arm came up to guard his head. The angry bull snorted and huffed, brayed and huffed, whimpered and huffed, sobbed and huffed, paused and sobbed, gasped and quieted. Would the next blow come in rage or tempered by gilt or laced with remorse? Herb's eyes were unwilling to explore the deafening silence that held the next unpredictable act in its clutches. His head and heart pounded. Were they audible to the attacker? Would blood cause additional frenzy? The quiet before a second assault on a passive, fetal shield, wasn't unwelcome. The fury remained at bay. Herb's own moaning filled the cubby of his curled-up world. Was the attack over? Was raw emotion finding reason? Would sorrow drive the assailant to stop? Herb's ears intimated the intruder invaded the opposite settee which huffed out air because a threatening boy fell on it. Herb refused to look into the brown eyes of anger.

His ears, however, hadn't any choice. Alvin cried. Sobs from across the gulf between these men begged, wanted, no demanded compassion. The surging outbursts cut through Herb's pain as he listened to torturous, self-punishing words. "Jesus," Alvin blurted like his Lord's name were a sharp blade for self-mutilation. "Alvin become his own pa," he moaned convulsively. Rebellious bawling came forth from Alvin, bawling held back in those merciless beatings back home in Georgia. Alvin forced out, "Beat his pretend lover just to beat the shit out of him."

"I'm okay," Herb blurted and found himself impulsively at Alvin's side as if a bull might befriend a matador before the kill. His arms hugged as if divested of mind-control, and Alvin's face sobbed hollowly against the bloody shirt of a man whose feelings were as genuine as both these raw hearts. "Please, Alvin. Please. I selfishly protected myself and didn't think—didn't think—God—I didn't think."

They rocked like a papa and wounded child. "Man," the boy cried, "Alvin done beat the shit out of you like my pa done—like my pa done me."

"I'm okay."

"Beat him like my pa done."

"You're a good man, Alvin."

"I be so sorry."

"I had it coming."

"Alvin don't deserve—"

"He deserves."

"I—I—can't stop sissy crying. So sorry, my pap.

"Please understand I love you."

"It just hard for me to be natural 'bout it."

"I know."

"Can friends still be friends?"

"Always."

They cradled together arm in arm. How long, Herb wasn't sure. Nor did he care about the time Alvin took to vent. In the deep, uncontrolled sobs, Herb felt the old man's backhand beat a frightened son mercilessly, heard the insults—*sissy, fag, mamma's boy, queer, homo*—hurled thoughtlessly, saw the bleeding a father's envy caused, smelled the inebriation used as whitewash, tasted the bitterness of monetary and patrimonial insecurity, and understood the toll of ungodly abuse. Survival sent Alvin to the white man's dumpster. Violence drove him from home. Determination sent him to a white man's university. Strength helped him thrive there. What bravery grew in a boy who drove his mother and siblings from Moultrie to Miami where he lost childhood becoming a surrogate dad? Didn't such courage deserve liberation? This moment of sympathy? This moment of love? An Afro nestled Herb's cheek, wetness soaked his sleeve, and heaves of emotion moved his arms. If one can ever rehearse friendship, fatherhood, or fraternity, Herb began in these minutes of liberation. Alvin slowly subdued himself as genuinely as he had freed intellect and talent from its handicapped background.

"Alvin liked to kill you."

"Are you okay now?"

"I be wiped out some like my own pa. What goes around, comes around."

"This time, I'll make the coffee. You're not driving home."

"You ain't okay with Alvin here." He stood and placed a palm on the ceiling above. Alvin shook his head to clear out a haze of Southern Comfort. A step and wobble brought his butt down gently on the table across from Herb. The deep brown eyes were bloodshot. Tears still sat on his cheeks. "I ain't—I mean—am not over the fits because my mind turns on what I just did. I am so ashamed. When Miss—ah—when Beth told me you lived on this boat, I never dreamed to see it like this."

"Did you ask, or did she volunteer my whereabouts?"

"Tonight is about you and me. I come—no—came to talk things out and got tight and angry. Being with you can't happen—I see that—but, Jesus, for my stretch with you, give some respect."

"Can we show mutual respect?"

"Okay."

"Herb owes me an apology."

"Here it is. I am sorry."

"A mite louder, Mr. Herb."

"I am truly sorry for behaving badly toward a friend."

"We still be pals?" he asked.

With that human belief—*always*—the story of Herb and Alvin came to rest, to a pleasant peace, to a wholesome closeness, a warranted closeness. Of course they would remain in touch with letters and phone calls and visits once Alvin moved to New York City where his future wanted him. Would love find him in his city of choice? As certainly and tempestuously as a creative spirit demanded. Would he ever know that he had a son named Jonas? More important, would Jonas ever be told about his papa? Letting it be known was Chris's call, not Herb's. If Alvin knew, he never shared that information with his lifelong buddy.

Chapter Twenty-Four

One Friday afternoon Lorraine asked if Herb minded dropping her off at the Biltmore Hotel on the way home. Coral Gables Players, a forerunner of the hotel's permanent regional theater, held auditions for *Separate Tables*, a two act play by Terence Rattigan. Lorraine would land the role of Miss Pat Cooper, a Bournemouth resort manager and fiancee of John Malcolm, a divorced alcoholic writer whose *ex* wife showed up at the Hotel Beauregard on purpose. While watching contender after contender vie for various roles, Herb noticed that the director eyed him. The thespian's glint of familiarity flaunted an unspoken line, "Haven't we met somewhere?" Focusing on the stage players to avoid eye contact, Herb disconcertingly noticed the man staring at him again. So continuous were the intrusive glances, they made Herb wait outside in the breeze way. It was infinitely less stressful but considerably more boring than watching the tryouts. Had he not agreed to wait for Lorraine, he'd certainly have gone for an afternoon cocktail at Friar Tucks. The languid afternoon in a hammock of slow moving clouds shaded the setting sun. Idle waiters copped smokes. There were scattered vehicles valets hadn't bothered to park. A drooping couple walked from sweat-slick tennis courts.

Without anything to read, he nearly decided to hit the hotel bar when a dwarf, a heavy jointed, quick-stepping girl told him that the director wished to see him. Determined the scenario should play out without his presence, he told the assistant to send Lorraine Shore to the hotel bar after her audition. The shrill, thin voice asked him to accompany her back to the auditions. As he turned to leave, she reluctantly informed him that the director wished him to read for the lead role. "John Malcolm in the flesh," was the phrase relayed through Howie's ambassador. For presenting a genuine "come on" line, the small girl sounded too indignant, too annoyed at bypassing fair tryout protocol which she probably worked to arrange. The pixie obviously felt her boss was off his rocker on this point.

Whether Herb read well or not made no difference to Howie who believed anyone could act as long as he or she looked the part. "I needed a Lawrence Harvey type, fella, for the roll," Howie said, "and, man, you're a dead ringer." So Herb agreed to play John Malcolm in *Separate Tables* directed by Howie Kwickton—the irony of the name brought a chuckle or two when Herb told the story. His acceptance came not from the need for new experiences, not because of latent exhibitionism, but because rehearsals would break off driving Lorraine home.

In New York community theaters, he'd played Mack the Knife in the "Three Penny Opera," Cauchon in "Joan of Arc," and some minor roles in "The Chalk Garden" and others. He worked to deliver an impressive performance as John Malcolm in the first act and as the phoney Major Pollock in the second. He liked playing opposite Lorraine as Miss Cooper, the hotel manager who loved John Malcolm and wished to become his wife. Herb became completely nonplused when the actress doing John Malcolm's *ex wife,* Ann Shankland, would quit weeks into rehearsal, and Beth Shockett, a member of the theater board and a friend of Howie Kwickton, would get the role. In his heart, Herb suspected foul play. In his heart, he believed Beth wished to play the other woman opposite him. Was Herb's relationship with Lorraine as shaky as Mr. Maclolm's and Miss Cooper's commitment to marry? *Separate Tables* was a vehicle because the role of a former wife coming to seduce her *ex* seemed too ironic and well-timed. At the announcement of the replacement, some cast members objected that Beth wasn't Actors' Equity. Howie asked if anyone in the cast would like to donate to the playhouse. And the next day, Beth showed up for rehearsals. Did she expect Herb to still dance to her music?

So here Herb stood—to be married to Miss Pat Cooper played by Lorraine Shore then plagued by the arrival at Bournemouth of his *ex wife,* a model, played by Beth Shockett. Was it any wonder that the ensemble delivered powerful performances night after night as the run extended for sell out audiences? Both the *Miami Herald* and the *Miami Daily News* gave the production rave reviews. "Herb Rizer, a Lawrence Harvey look alike, carries emotional authority in the role of John Malcolm," one reviewer wrote. "Director Howie Kwickton's casting of Lorraine Shore and Beth Shockett as rivals for the love of one man, made the evening worth my time and yours, dear reader," wrote another.

It wasn't difficult for Herb to imagine himself as a sot especially in the love scene with his *ex*. He wondered how many performances Dr. Samuel Shockett sat through and watched the tumultuous kissing scene. Thank God Peter stood down when he embraced Beth as Ann Shankland. The drawn-out kiss pleased the director and the audience who believed in its revitalizing authenticity. Even Lorraine wondered about the electrifying pleasure the actors presented. But playing a drunk engaged to Lorraine Shore as Pat Cooper had all to do with his new found interest. At the conclusion of *Separate Tables,* Lorraine Shore as Pat Cooper got left in the lurch as Herb Rizer as John Malcolm reunited with his old flame, Beth Shockett as Ann Shankland. Of course, Herb wished to re-write the ending because he had no intension of letting Beth, who played the part of a despairing lover with overwhelming aplomb, control his heart anymore.

Chapter Twenty-Five

The theater costume room became a catalyst for new complications in Herb's life. The director, Howie Kwickton—fast with things besides stage directing, understood the requisites of his actors emotional needs. He provided seclusion for them during down time. While polishing a scene with Beth Shockett as Ann Shankland, he gave a long break and the key to the costume closet to Herb as John Malcolm and Major Pollack and Lorraine as Pat Cooper and Sybil and asked them to select wardrobes. The room contained rows of racked clothing, stacked flats, containers of supplemental stage lights, piled furniture, hung yet jumbled tools, shelves of paint and supplies, bolts of burlap and cloth, a display case with costume jewelry, and boxes of hats and shoes. The overhead florescents, though, brightened the room so that costumes and theater gear had nowhere to hide. Rummaging through racks of costumes, Herb found a tzarina-style, white gown and arm's length gloves to match and helped Lorraine dress in them. For himself, he selected a tailed tuxedo, top hat, and gold-tipped cane. They looked exquisite in the valet mirror set in a corner. Herb bowed like a court herald and announced in noble, royal tenor, "We humbly present Tzarina Rokmaninov, sovereign of all Russia and the Baltics, Grand Duchess of Estonia." He extended a hand, "Your royal highness, welcome to the ball," and the monarch in pure, white grandeur haughtily floated toward her gallant. Like very-important-persons leading off a state affair, they waltzed to Herb singing "Sweet While it Lasted," from the Three Penny Opera. They twirled in what little space the storeroom offered its royalty as a crowded dance floor and then flamboyantly waltzed down isles of clothing. Lorraine's performance as empress was more lavish than Herb's singing, and he had a damn good voice she told him at the end of the dance.

Re-racking the costumes, Lorraine wore only the long,

white gloves, a rayon slip, panty hose, and pumps; Herb, only a shirt, briefs, socks, and loafers. Racing through the hanging garments looking for John Malcolm's and Pat Cooper's wardrobes, they each held up possibilities which, with nods of approval, were draped over the racks. When Herb donned an olive, double-breasted, twilled gaberdine suit with wide lapels Lorraine clapped and told him that John Malcolm obviously bought it at Austin Reed in London. She donned a pink fringed chemise and red feather boa without a trace of Miss Cooper in the outfit. Herb chuckled and remarked on its gay-nineties, bordello flavor. That got her singing, "Let Me Entertain You," from *Gypsy* to which she did a Gypsy Rose Lee impersonation and mock striptease by removing a long glove and twirling it. When she wound the feather boa around his neck and led him through the racks, he tossed off his jacket, she, a glove, he, pants, she, the chemise, he, the dress shirt, she, her slip until a divan found them embraced and petting.

"I'm a virgin," she said.

"I'm not," he said.

"Your moves hint at that." She smiled audaciously.

"Those pantyhose will protect your virginity."

She raised her wonderfully round hips and slipped them down.

"I've eaten from the tree of good and evil," he said.

Her smile unveiled glistening, model teeth which opened with a gentle nudge from his tongue. Lorraine winced as if French kissing posed a mystery to her intimacy. Yet she coated his alighting like nectar from a flower. "Oh, Herb, your tenderness fascinates me. I trust in your gentleness," she whispered.

"And I, in yours."

Herb felt unclear about virginity during his staging. Knowledge came from school-buddy chat and off-handed, locker room jokes, but he sensed that Lorraine wished no more rehearsal time. In the rising action, she guided him to honest and powerful performance. And he eased into the role like a veteran. Because of tightness, he reached dramatic

149

conclusion well before his desire for mutual gratification. Lorraine moaned, panted, whimpered, and went to kissing, rubbing, hugging—a wondrous curtain call—just as a member of the audience threw a paint bucket on the concrete floor. The thud broke the passionate scene. Herb jerked his head up. Lorraine gasped. Beth Shockett stood third row, orchestra center from the drama on the divan. "For God's sake," she announced, "get the hell dressed, you two," and stormed out on the curtain call.

Chapter Twenty-Six

Minnie regularly raised the topic with Herb of settling down and making grandchildren. Lunching with her, an unmarried son became antsy across from his mother at a Bayside table inside the California style Rusty Pelican on Key Biscayne. Getting to the restaurant across the Rickenbacker Causeway was easier now that a scandal-beleaguered *Tricky Dick* abused his power ruthlessly, retaliated against critics, threatened the special prosecutor, and had little time for this tropical island retreat. Herb rued the coming matrimony plea, but discussing politics got him angry because of Minnie's one-note retort, "Richard Nixon is our country's president, right or wrong." It made no difference if Herb pointed out the illegal bombing of Cambodia, plans to assassinate columnist Jack Anderson, selling arms clandestinely, accepting illegal campaign contributions, probable guilt in a coverup, rumors of recorded anti Jewish comments made in the oval office, and generally acting like a monarch instead of the president of a democratic society. She'd counter with, he ended the war and made friends with the Chinese to which Herb would respond heatedly about the rising number of homeless Americans. *President right or wrong.* So he kept a lid on opinions as Minnie played with her ususal Pompano Almondine by cutting tiny pieces so that the fish couldn't be reserved just as a table-side waiter prepared a caesar salad for Herb. Awaiting the inevitable inquiry, Herb watched carefully as the server broke a raw egg into the romaine lettuce, pressed in fresh garlic, drenched olive oil around, squeezed in fresh lemon, and began to toss it. As many times as Herb had observed the preparation, he'd been unable to recreate the salad Rusty Pelican Style. Anchovies, grated Parmesan, and fresh ground pepper—what the hell did he forget that made the caesar salad on his boat taste mediocre? He was served a sample, and the damn caesar tasted uncommonly delicious. After the waiter plated it and walked off, the probe began. "A mother's patience wears thin waiting for my youngest to say he's getting married," Minnie started.

"At twenty-six are my practice years over, Ma?"

"You're not getting any younger."

"I'm working toward my doctorate in love."

"Why did you bring Lorraine to lunch last time. Is there something I should know?"

"Did you construe her tagging along as an ad for bridal gowns?"

"*Oy*, I'm laughing on the outside but crying on the inside. I'm afraid Lorraine is just a pacifier for a worried-mother, you know, an accommodation, a show, window dressing for who knows what."

"Are you being intentionally caustic and indirect?"

"Alvonica McKinnon tells me you and Alvin are two peas in a pod."

"Where are you going with this lead in, which I might add, infringes on my privacy?"

"You're my son. People talk."

"Eat your fish. About what?"

"A certain director and department head, I think you know who, spent a week on a boat with a music teacher *shikseh* and a student *faigeleh*."

"On what other looming scandals can you shed *Yiddisheh* wisdom?"

"Don't make fun of your mother. You drink in bars. So drunk Alvin drove you home and spent the night."

"Very old news. You're just now finding out?"

"An unpleasant past leads to a troubled future."

"Can we discuss something else?"

"If Alvin is trouble, I can help. Tell me."

"I see Chris gave you some spicy material for our lunch chat."

"Now, I'm not saying who, but is what she said true?"

"It all sounds a bit much coming from a mother's point of view. By the way, Alvonica wants you to get involved in *A Raisin in the Sun*. It would be good for you to work on something you love to do."

"Don't change the subject. Lorraine likes you. I see it in her eyes."

"Mom. I like her too."

"So?"

"I don't know."

"Are you scared?"

"Of love, yes."

"Why?"

"Because it's a weapon in someone else's hand."

"Because of your father and me? You know our disagreements always forced us closer when we got back together. Hardship I sent his way, but he loved me for a lifetime, endlessly. And I loved him, God rest his soul, despite myself. Herbie, love is a trolley car you run after even if it won't stop."

"Did I ever tell you that Sol and Minnie created the best love story for two sons? Jake and Jenny have a great marriage, and your granddaughter Brett dotes on you."

"What about my Herbie? Shouldn't he share some happiness?"

"He does."

"Your mother wants you to find yourself."

"I'm not lost."

"And to have contentment. She doesn't care if you love a girl or a *goy,* I mean boy as long as my son is happy. That's all I ask before I die."

"Enjoy your lunch, Minnie, and don't plan to die too soon."

Did the raw confession at that lunch in the Rusty Pelican and the off-stage activity during *Separate Tables* prompt Herb to seriously think about Lorraine as a significant other? *Think*, perhaps, wasn't the correct word. He was at ease with Lorraine, enjoyed her company, marveled at her mystery, saw her beauty both inside and out, wanted to protect and help her, savored her audacious, continual smile; liked her humor, her intellect, her impeccable taste, attention to style and fashion; appreciated her humor, laughed with her about philosophical aversions to

153

perspiration, sports, all gymnastics, camping, sailing (she didn't swim, but Herb was sure that would change in time); and found her admitted clumsiness endearing. When he took her sailing on his movable home, she took to day sailing on the *Sea Witch* and eventually to over-nighters like a good sport. What did it matter if her love-making was flat. With experience, she'd likely become creative.

The bad news came in the form of Beth Shockett. What she faced, no, walked out on during the Gables Theater rehearsal evidently set her off. She likely prompted the bad publicity appearing in the *Miami Herald* article profiling Dr. Samuel Shockett for his work at Miami Children's Hospital and his development of a spinal fusion for congenital, spinal abnormalities. Toward the end of the in depth interview, Dr. Shockett lambasted taxpayer monies going to liberal hokum like the university's college within a college led by it's Director, Herb Rizer. Fund medical research, the good doctor stated, where the money was sorely needed to save lives. Was it unkind of Herb to believe hubby's criticism came from conversations with the good doctor's wife? Was it merely loss of control or also what his wife witnessed on a divan in a costume room that tagged the doctor's opinion as planted and not his own?

Both the *Miami Herald* and the *Miami Daily News* sent reporters to Herb's doorstep the day following the article in Sunday's paper. And neither the man nor the woman reporter seemed interested in a progressive program's successes. Herb showed each reporter the open, interdisciplinary laboratories, encouraged them to interview students about their learning progress, shared early graduation statistics and acceptances into graduate programs at ivy league universities which used graduate exam scores and Miami's professional evaluations in lieu of grades and grade-point averages, bragged about a non-existent drop out and failure rate, asked them to interview teaching administrators including the dean of music, dean of Arts and Sciences, and President Beaumont himself who taught statistical analysis in the program, suggested they also look

154

at the interaction between professors and students in the student union, conference rooms, and offices. He opened to both reporters records of cost effectiveness ratios (students to staff, spending per student), invited them to talk to faculty about differentiated staffing, and presented accolades from professional journals and prominent, national periodicals citing the outstanding experimental program. The *Miami Herald* ran a "Neighbors" back page column about advances in modern education. What the *News* wrote about was federal funding to prop up an experimental boondoggle that would die of its own volition once the financial backing dried up.

Unfortunately, the reporter from the *News* followed up with a visit to Lola May Ferringer. The vice-president, of course, repeated the mantra of educational basics, funding for medical research, engineering, and the sciences, and security deficiencies on campus. When the *Miami Daily News* reporter returned to Herb's office, she asked for a copy of ethics and morality standards for college faculty. What policies were in place to regulate professors fraternizing with students, did the university screen employees for infractions of the law or for arrest records, were sexual deviants permitted to work around or with students, did academic freedom mean no holds barred in discussions and assignments criticizing social mores, and so on? Herb, who backed the initiative to pass Dade County's gay rights, anti discrimination legislation, thought the reporter's hidden agenda was an underpin of vocal right-wing celebrities like Anita Bryant, Miss Florida Orange Juice for family values.

Then, when the former interim English department head was arrested in a men's room at Crandon Park for lewd and lascivious behavior all hell broke loose in the press. *Charles Boyd, tenured professor of English at the University of Miami and former department head, was arraigned in county court today on morals . . . . These aberrants seek converts to their lifestyle. Shouldn't our families have rights? Deviants on Miami's campus charged with kids' education must be terminated.* Out of jail on his own recognizance pending trial, Boyd was dismissed by Lola May Ferringer who found herself in a squeeze when Dr. Beaumont overrode her decision and placed the man on suspension with pay. She tap-danced around the issue in a subsequent visit from the *Miami Daily News* by stating her dismissal only took away teaching duties, interaction with students until his matter was settled. She apologized for any misunderstandings due to her use of the word *dismissed* and assured the press she and Dr. Beaumont were on the same page in this unfortunate incident.

Next, the tabloid press indicted the Dean of Arts and Sciences, Abraham Alvarez, for frequenting an off-color club, Compadres, and demanded his immediate resignation. Someone had passed a photo of the dean dancing among a group of men, some bare-chested, one in a Speedo. The *News* ran a local front page headline with the photograph, "Who's Playing with Miami's Youth." And channel seven cameras and anchor Wayne Farris were on campus like flies on manure. When the dean refused to comment, Farris found an English-stumbling, Latin janitor to admit that the dean "walk to Rumba music in his head all the day." The dean held on to his roller coaster position at Herb's insistence and with his loyal support. To alleviate the media frenzy, Herb contacted the Anti-Defamation League of the B'nai B'rith and appealed to them for a stand against the *News* and channel seven for slander. Rabbi Kaplan, at Herb's insistence, pressured the local ADL chapter which wrote a position paper partially published in *The Miami Herald,* "The ADL does not promote nor condone homosexual lifestyles, but it is dedicated to the protection of minorities' civil rights and for individuals to work and live in a discrimination free environment."

The *Herald* quoted the rabbi's rebuke of the *Miami Daily News's* yellow journalism and Wayne Ferris's inflammatory television report. Herb also asked the American Civil Liberties Union to file a suit against the paper. He secretly retained a prominent local attorney, Ellis Rubin, to monitor events and/or take legal action on behalf of the dean.

President Beaumont came under fire for defending his

institution in a statement released to *The Miami Herald* against unwarranted witch hunts and blasted the *Miami Daily News* for its biased reporting. The paper fired back with a scathing expose of Beaumont's inability to keep pace with a growing institution and suggested that the president worked years beyond his need to retire. The expose' cited misappropriated funds in the athletic department, deteriorating and unsafe dorms, mishandling of narcotics and other medications at the campus's hospital, suggested that research grants were used to build a new band room and music library, and furthermore *The News* resurrected from its morgue a yesteryear rape of a male jogger on campus by six females—five students and one university security officer—as incompetently handled by Beaumont. The Molina Case as it came to be known had been rerun before to help a local attorney rocket to national prominence, and now, years after its freshness, used to make or break another reputation. The story prompted the university's board of directors to buy out Beaumont's contract and to force him to step down immediately. When the president acquiesced, Lola May Ferringer became interim head of the university. And Herb was not far down on her hit list.

One of President Ferringer's first moves to bring the university in line with sound educational practice was to cut off funding for guest speakers, visiting artists, the university press, community outreach programs, student exchanges, visiting faculty. She severely slashed the budgets of drama, film study, communications, graphic and performing arts, badminton, swimming, women's tennis and volleyball, jazz, choral music, and psychology. A good portion of the funds went for increased campus security, remodeling executive offices, secretarial and support staff, a massive landscape thrust, and computer equipment. Medical research received her firm handshake. She split, reorganized, and combined deans' responsibilities which cost the music school dean his job. With the lawsuit filed on Max Alvarez's behalf, she feared tampering with Arts and Sciences but reduced his jurisdiction by shifting several disciplines into Humanities including the English department. She replaced Herb as its head with a professor on special assignment and without additional salary. She established dress code standards for students and faculty, threatened the expulsion of sororities and fraternities for infractions of moral propriety—Zeta, Bata Tau and Sigma Chi were closed down and the university reclaimed their campus houses and land. She advocated the use of graduate students to teach undergraduate classes and filled vacancies with part time adjuncts who were offered no standard benefits. Before the academic year was out, recruiters from Northwestern, Antioch, Juliard, Amhearst, University of California, University of North Carolina, and others lured some of Miami's best professors away.

Obviously she did nothing about Herb's directorship due to the federal grant which supported the college within a college. Herb declined an offer to return to Hunter as its registrar, an offer from Columbia to teach administration and supervision, and an offer from Rollins College to head its Humanities Program. For a number of reasons, he turned down the jobs: he'd signed a four year contract with the federal government for his program; he wished to grow the program's strengths and tighten its loose ends; he loved teaching; he'd come home to Miami for a parent's heath once and his mother wasn't getting any younger; he felt obligated to Max Alvarez; he loved sailing and living aboard the *Sea Witch*; and Lorraine and Miami went together. Besides, Ferringer was merely an interim head of state and an old woman as well. And the university board formed an exploratory committee to present candidates after a national search. So he bet on outlasting her reign and her rear view mirror educational philosophy.

158

What Ferringer did do to Herb's domain was to schedule rooms so that his faculty taught as far from one another as possible on a sixty or so acre campus. She overloaded his support staff by reassigning personnel who received part or all their salary from internal funds. All teaching administrator classes were dissolved and their students foisted onto now overloaded faculty. Ferringer demanded federal grant money reimburse the general fund for utilities, office space, classroom usage, supplies and copying, and further informed professors that publications created by them became the intellectual property of the University of Miami. The latter edict caused a Harvard mathematician and a Fullbright historian to move on to campuses out of state.

Those good educators who stayed felt philosophically committed to progressive ideas and believed that the reactionary reign was temporary. Under Herb's leadership, indeed, the college within a college withstood the Ferringer onslaught mainly because of viable educational strategies which fostered student progress and academic success. Classroom energy and good teaching is, for a while, immune to negative politics.

The Hurricane, U of M's student paper ran favorable press for the progressive cause every week. Several staff writers were in the program. Student activists, well aware of the attack on the college within a college, mustered a weak but effective demonstration when President Ferringer spoke at the Tiger Bay Club. *The Miami Herald* headline went, "U of M President Clashes with Student Protestors," and quoted Ferringer's stance, "The University of Miami's traditional courses of study with a reduction in marginal, costly programs ruffles a vocal fringe at home and on other major campuses nation wide. But our vital institution will carry on as a strong educational force in Florida and America under our watch." An interview with the protest organizer, Alvin

McKinnon, stated that a new group, Citizens for Quality Education, protested increased tuition at a time when the university slashed financial aid, scholarships, work-study, and viable educational programs. In addition, the president hired part time adjuncts and beginners to replace notable, tenured professors.

The protest garnered support among community progressives particularly from Mensa and its spokesman, Dr. Geoffrey Curry. Endorsements of the college within a college came from local institutions and religious leaders—Pastor Roeby Williamson and The First Baptist Church, the Methodist Church of Miami, Temple Emanu El, the school board, the Drama Guild of Greater Miami—these helped morale and checked the Ferringer dismantling. Although Herb maintained a low profile during the controversy, he knew the Eustis Harpy was piqued by pressures brought to bear on her. Yet Ferringer intervened further the following year and appointed Beth Shockett as co-director of Herb's program. She split its faculty down the middle in terms of administrative responsibility.

The first meeting between co-directors focused more on items other than budget or program needs or faculty or how the director's space might be modified or how Herb's personal secretary would be shared. When Beth Shockett came into the staff-shared room that Friday afternoon, faculty, students, aids, the secretary, and other support staff trickled out during the cool greetings between co-directors. The headquarters usually buzzed with activity until near dinnertime—the discussion, argument, discourse, interaction, exchange of teachers and learners, mentors and proteges, evaluators and creators was continual. Ferringer's new appointee looked around as the room became vacant.

Herb began, "I hope working with you will be more fruitful than knowing you, Mrs. Shockett."

"Herb, I—"

"Mr. Rizer, if you please."

"Your work moved this institution to the forefront. I'm honored to work in this family of progressives."

"We've become stepchildren."

"I hate what the newspapers—hate myself for—"

"Please, Mrs. Shockett, tell me how you wish this space divided."

"Here are the specification." She slipped a legal manilla envelop across his desk.

"I think you'll find that this program directs itself."

"A testimony to your talents, Mr. Rizer. But the president specifically asked for a division of faculty supervision."

"Division will hurt the program. I suggest you submit your proposal to the faculty steering committee."

"The president reassigned the committee solely to community affairs."

"Is your machine gun aimed at anything else?"

"Lorraine Shore."

"On what grounds?"

"Moral impropriety."

"I wouldn't go there if I were you."

"Is that a threat?"

"Yes."

"Ferringer arranged a position for her at the junior college in Opa Locka."

"Isn't it time we called a truce."

"Dr. Beaumont's out of the picture. The dean of music is gone. Max Alvarez fights for his life. Alvin graduates in June. Please, Herb, you're the kiss of death to anyone who defends you or whom you defend."

"Convince Ferringer to lay off Lorraine—that is if she even cares—or I'll find a way to arrange a position for you at Miami Edison High School."

Not long after the co-directors set up shop and the program survived the new division, Herb sat in the throne room of Lola May Ferringer, President of the University of Miami. This time her walls held an impressive array of award winning artwork presented to Dr. Beaumont from juried shows held by the Art Department. The only eyesore among the sculpted pieces and tastefully framed canvasses was the blowup of Boman F. Ashe. Ferringer wore the same clash of colors as when they first met in an interview for the registrar's job. She informed him that the university bought out his contract and in June he was free to pursue another career. He told her that he'd make no trouble if she laid off of Lorraine Shore. Ferringer said she was shocked to learn that such a valued professor as Miss Shore might consider leaving U of M. Herb should have guessed that new employees' low salaries would be more important to the new president than any petty squabble of a jealous malcontent. Beth's gun had been loaded with blanks.

Chapter Twenty-Eight

One task that both Rizer brothers never wished to assume was to run a father's business. The conglomerate had its roots in Miami's gambling era of the twenties and Herb never cared for nefarious business associates with whom his father dealt. His dad's ownership of the Five O'clock Club came about through the good graces of mobster Longy Zwillman, and Sol got out from under the wings of Meyer Lansky when Herb's Uncle Abe resumed shakedowns. But life at the university, an ivory tower sheltered from riffraff, had its own nefarious types. And a guy could be far less disappointed with questionable businessmen than with ignoble educators. Thus far, because of handpicked and trusted caretakers, the Rizer family business fared well. But like his father, these executives were older men and women near or past retirement age. And major decisions had been forestalled by Sol's death. Some of the hotels needed complete renovations; the Five O'clock Club lost money because of competitive franchises; Miami Beach cited Rizer Enterprises with code and safety violations because an influential developer vied for the Sheri Frontinac as a condo conversion; the manager of the Beau Rivage, on sick leave, wished to retire; an eminent domain case against some blocks of stores and apartments on Miami Beach needed attention, as well as other complications that Minnie was unable to manage. Herb decided, therefore, that at the school year's end, instead of taking other offers in education, he'd take on Rizer Enterprises.

On a Sunday during finals, Herb went to the office to pack files, books, and personal things. The task had been put off too long because his heart wasn't in it. Several colleagues and Alvin begged him to stay and fight. Dean Alvarez, vindicated by the ADL, was foolishly willing to take on Ferringer. Dr. Geoffrey Curry was crestfallen by Herb's contract buyout and cutbacks in the arts. He offered Herb a financial assault on the institution to use as he wished.

Lorraine's advice was heartfelt. She said to do what was best for him, and that's what Herb went with. He chose to reorganize the family business, run it smoothly and profitably, and then liquidate it. His career choices would remain on hold until then.

His mother still hounded him about fearing life. He'd loved and lost Mary in a whirlwind of bigotry. He'd loved and lost Beth in a whirlwind of emotion. Yet he'd moved on from the unmarked grave of their relationships. He'd failed as a middle man for Chris though he'd kept his promise to drive her to Plymouth. He'd seen Jonas when she returned to live with her parents who cared for the infant so Chris might resume her duties at the university. There was a grand wedding at the First Baptist Church where she gave her hand to Reverend Roeby Williamson who seemed a happy dad and husband.

Although Lorraine had offered packing help, he hadn't shared a time or date with her mainly because of the need to be alone while compacting this overcharged chapter of his life. Hadn't she done a good turn by organizing a sendoff at the Rusty Pelican with students and faculty? Hadn't they roasted him with love and humor? Hadn't they presented a heartfelt film documenting years, though too few, of their beloved program with him as their leader? Hadn't his students presented him with an autographed scrapbook and a plaque? Everyone had done enough, yet Alvin insisted on getting a friend and carting the packed memorabilia in his truck to a prearranged storage facility. Organized packing was a depressing and solitary task anyway.

Once most personal effects were boxed, Herb sat at his old desk. Going through unopened mail, he found a letter from The University of Chicago, Office of the Dean, which read,

> *Dear Mr. Rizer,*
>
> *Recently we asked our new graduate students if, during their undergraduate years, they were fortunate enough to have had a teacher whom they considered outstanding and inspiring. You will be pleased to*

know that one of your former students has identified you as the best teacher of his undergraduate years. He has especially commended your provision of a most stimulating learning atmosphere—and your special skills in teaching others the art of writing and reporting all through your evident delight in the English language . . . .

Although there were several more paragraphs, Herb found himself slumped down with his forehead on his forearm, his eyes stubbornly wet, and his throat filled with emotion. He cried for good friendships, good fortune, happy and sad times, cried for leaving behind his successes and mistakes, despaired at the trouble brought upon Max Alvarez, felt bad about the loss of music's Dean Bitter, wept for lost love, for found love, and cried because his mind insisted on stupid blubbering as closure for energies expended on this campus with students he loved. The end of his teaching career seemed almost as traumatic as the loss of his dad. And this move was an ending. He felt that. Accepting Ferringer's walking papers was the act of a coward, the surrender of dreams, the sad loss of purpose, but he was sick of contention, tired of trying to out-wait fate, angry at the attacks on a viable program. The Eustis Harpy had won; close allies and loyal backers of an avant garde program had lost; Herb had lost; progressive ideas, like passe Jack Roses, went down the drain of basic education. Besides, federal funding ended this coming fall semester, and reality dictated that the college within a college would be history unless, unless—oh, what the hell.

When he heard a key turn in lock on the office door, he stood and faced away staring through a window overlooking the tropical commons. He thought of Dr. Beaumont's reign of growth for the university brought to an untimely end. He thought of professors, good teachers, transferring from Miami. Beaumont brought a new center for international studies, a four story monolith that filled once open space. Ferringer brought islands of mulched plants now replacing lawns where students had gathered and chatted, their former debating places judiciously shaped into unusable space. New concrete benches, like bus stops on a rural highway, sat sporadically along walkways. Pruned trees had low ground cover and hedges around them to keep people from loitering in their shade. The newly remodeled Ashe Administration Building sported a fresh coat of beige and brown paint which contrasted starkly with its pressure cleaned, coral rock facade. New air conditioning units spit their condensation into special drains which dumped algae into the lake. The water had lost its emerald quality since the manmade fountain had been shut down. Emergency phones stood like sentries along tarmac paths which crossed the commons to faded classroom buildings. Thunder heads blocked the morning sun as a security guard exited his new booth and headed for an empty parking lot. What had once been familiar transformed into the alien in a short span of time, he thought. Change was what Herb brought to this campus and change had become its double edged blade.

Heels clicked on the terrazzo floor as someone approached from behind. Not predisposed to face the Sunday newcomer, he found comfort in the darkening sky, the rumble of distant thunder, and a flash of lightening which caused the overhead lights to flicker. Yet when she spoke, Herb knew immediately who invaded his packing privacy.

"Will you be going back to New York?"

When he turned, she stopped in front of the desk in one of those diaphanous dresses that once usurped his attention. How unfashionable and matronly it appeared now. The adorable long, blond hair had been cropped to shoulder length. And crows feet and wrinkled brows marked time which she'd believed wasn't her ally. He felt invaded yet wasn't at all angry.

Once Beth had been flattered by his arousal on a bench outside the Faculty Club, pleased that her presence stirred him. Once she'd vowed, "I love you," yet remarried a man she felt at ease to betray. The tables had turned, irony come full circle as Herb felt a distant flattery because of her

166

envy, jealousy, anger at what she'd discovered in a costume room at the Biltmore theater. He felt no animosity either. Beth's intrusion on his program wasn't her doing. It was Ferringer's. Who was responsible for the destructive nature of a vindictive president? Not the English lit prof who had been nearly as used and abused as Herb.

"I hadn't intended for us to end this way," she said.

"I understand. In which scene did you envision us ending? The motel room scene? The restraining order scene? Your wedding scene? The shared office scene? The costume room scene?"

"Please forgive me."

"No need. It took both of us to muddle this."

"I feel so—so—"

"Don't."

"You've been crying."

"An oncoming cold is all."

"Always and ever the bad liar."

"Consider that I've just accepted endings."

"Are we ended then, you and I?"

"Herb is."

"What if Beth isn't?"

"Sad. I'd say just as you did, we're even."

"We loved beyond understanding."

"I once thought so."

"I think about—"

"I don't anymore."

"Are a man's feelings so changeable?"

"When you bury a lover, the hurt decays."

"Show me a grave, and I'll gladly pay my last respects."

"Respect my office and my program. It's yours now. My confederates sat *shiveh* at the Rusty Pelican last night."

"Do you see any man wanting me as much as you do?"

"Did you show up here to live unfortunate history?"

"Imagine that I still hope."

"I'm flattered."

She stood before him like an alabaster statue of memory, and her stance appeared as awkward as the first day she showed him through the English offices and sized him up as an experiment divorcees conduct without regard for collateral damage. He hadn't any questions to ask because he didn't want any answers. If he'd been played for love's fool, he wished for no revelations. A marked up copy of *Separate Tables* he placed in the box with other memorabilia and resumed packing as if the female statue in a diaphanous dress might be put away with other stuff. Continued his work until the alabaster work of art, once his Galatea, retreated through a violated doorway out of his life. Buried in his heart, Herb bore scars that the inexperienced take to their graves, held memories which teach caution. He knew that what Beth had done, Lorraine wouldn't do. He understood why life before Lorraine had merely been practice for a strong future, one where love grows with wisdom not with wild abandon. He picked up the phone, dialed, and asked if he might pick his girl up for dinner and a movie, thought about the ring his mother had given him, a family heirloom, a remaining vestige of the grandeur of the Rizer's roots in Russia. It was time, he felt, that his doctorate in love were put to lasting use.

www.ingramcontent.com/pod-product-compliance
Lightning Source LLC
Chambersburg PA
CBHW051239170626
46809CB00004B/1394